A muscle flexed in the plane of his cheek, just to the side of his scar. 'I'm only human, and my basic human needs are no different to anyone else's.'

It took Ailsa a couple of seconds to find her voice after that incendiary comment, because she was busy fielding the giant wave of hurt that washed over her at the idea of Jake having his sexual needs met by another woman... maybe even *more* than one woman. They'd been divorced for four years now, after all, and it was hardly the first time the thought had crossed her mind. Most times she quickly pushed it away. But she intimately knew her husband's needs in that department.

'What about *my* needs?' she asked, struggling to keep her voice level. 'Do I have the same freedom there as you do, Jake? Or don't you think I have such needs any more, since the accident rendered me unable to bear children? Perhaps you think it's made me less of a woman?'

The day **Maggie Cox** saw the film version of *Wuthering Heights*, with a beautiful Merle Oberon and a very handsome Laurence Olivier, was the day she became hooked on romance. From that day onwards she spent a lot of time dreaming up her own romances, secretly hoping that one day she might become published and get paid for doing what she loved most! Now that her dream is being realised, she wakes up every morning and counts her blessings. She is married to a gorgeous man, and is the mother of two wonderful sons. Her two other great passions in life—besides her family and reading/writing—are music and films.

Recent titles by the same author:

SURRENDER TO HER SPANISH HUSBAND
SECRETARY BY DAY, MISTRESS BY NIGHT
BRAZILIAN BOSS, VIRGIN HOUSEKEEPER

THE LOST WIFE

BY
MAGGIE COX

First published in Great Britain 2011
by Mills & Boon, an imprint of Harlequin (UK) Limited,
Eton House, 18-24 Paradise Road, Richmond, Surrey TW9 1SR

© Maggie Cox 2011

ISBN: 978 0 263 22095 7

THE LOST WIFE

CHAPTER ONE

SHE ran to the window when she heard the muffled engine sound of the car coming up the drive. When it pulled up in front of the cottage, the smart silver-grey SUV that belonged to her ex-husband looked like a snowmobile, blanketed in several layers of thick white frosting. And still the crystalline flakes fell relentlessly from the sky, as if poured through some divine sieve.

The snowy display hadn't let up all day. Ailsa would have succumbed to the magic of it if she hadn't been so concerned about Jake returning their daughter safely home. Living in an English country idyll had lots to commend it, but when severe winter weather kicked in the hilly narrow roads could be utterly treacherous. She stood waiting with the front door open as the driver of the vehicle stepped out and walked across the snow-laden path towards her.

It wasn't Alain—the slim, smart-suited chauffeur she'd been expecting. Usually it was Jake's French driver that brought Saskia home from her fortnightly trips to London to visit her father, or from the airport when Jake was working in Copenhagen and she stayed with him there. When Ailsa saw the once familiar diamond-chipped blue eyes staring back at her through the relentlessly falling snow, her heart stalled.

'Hi,' he said.

She hadn't seen her ex-husband face to face in a long time...not since his chauffeur had become a reliable go-between. The impact of confronting those carved, unforgettable features hadn't lessened one iota, she discovered. He'd always had the kind of effortlessly handsome looks that guaranteed major female interest wherever he went. *Even with the cruel scar that ran down his cheekbone.* In truth, it made his already compelling visage utterly and disturbingly memorable—and *not* just because his beautiful face carried such a vivid wound. But the sight of that wound now made Ailsa's heart pound and her stomach clench with remembered sorrow at how it had occurred.

For a long moment she got lost in the dark cavern of memory, then realised that Jake was staring at her, waiting for her greeting. 'Hello...it's been a long time, Jake.'

Even as she spoke, she was thinking he should have warned her that there'd been a change of plan.

Her insides jolted. 'Where's Saskia?'

'I've been trying to ring you all day but there's been no damn signal! Why in God's name you would choose to live out here in the middle of nowhere is beyond me.'

Ignoring the irritation in his voice, which bisected her heart with knives, Ailsa pushed back her hair and crossed her arms over her thick Arran sweater. Just standing on the doorstep inside the peg-tiled porch, she was already freezing from the blast of icy air that had hit her when she'd opened the door.

'Has something happened? Why isn't Saskia with you?' Peering over his shoulder at the snow-covered vehicle, she willed herself to see her daughter's pretty heart-shaped face staring back at her through a window—*any* window so long as she was there. When she realised the car was empty the bones in her legs morphed into limp spaghetti.

'That's what I've been trying to call you about. She

wanted to stay with her grandmother in Copenhagen for a while…she pleaded with me to let her stay until Christmas Eve. I agreed. Because she was worried that you might be upset about that I agreed to travel here myself and give you the news. I'd heard the weather was bad but I had no idea it was as grim as this.'

His hand impatiently swept the snow from his champagne-blond hair, but the white flakes quickly settled again to render the gesture pointless. For a long moment Ailsa couldn't summon the words to reply. Shock and disappointment rolled through her in a sickening hurtful wave as she thought of all the plans she'd made for the lead-up to Christmas Day with Saskia. *The plans that now wouldn't be materialising.*

They'd been going to make a special trip to London for shopping, then stay at a nice hotel for the night so they could go to the theatre and out to dinner. Only yesterday the Norwegian pine she'd ordered had arrived, and was standing bare and alone in the living room just waiting for the shiny baubles that would transform it into a magical seasonal emblem. Mother and daughter were going to decorate it together, with carols playing joyfully in the background either on a CD or from the radio. It was inconceivable that her beloved child wouldn't be home again until Christmas Eve.

In Ailsa's mind the days leading up to that date would only serve to remind her of how lonely she could feel without the family she had once counted upon… *Jake and Saskia…* She'd barely got through the past week without Saskia as it was.

'How could you do this to me? How? You and your mother have already had her staying with you for a week! You must know that I was counting on you bringing her back today.'

The broad shoulders beneath the stylish black overcoat now smothered in snow shrugged laconically. 'Would you deny our daughter the chance to be with her grandmother when she's so recently lost my father? Saskia lifts her spirits like no other human being can.'

Knowing her daughter's warm, bubbly nature, Ailsa didn't doubt her ex-husband's words. But it didn't make her absence any easier to bear. And underneath her frustration her heart constricted at the thought that Jake's father was gone. The senior Jacob Larsen had been imposing, and even a little intimidating, but he had always treated her with the utmost respect. When Saskia had arrived in the world he hadn't stinted on his praise, proclaiming his new granddaughter to be the most beautiful baby in the world.

How sad for his son that he was gone. Their relationship had had its challenges, but there was no doubt in her mind that Jake had loved his father.

The swirling snow that was rapidly turning into a blizzard added to her misery and distress. 'I'm sorry you lost your dad…he was a good man. But I've already endured Saskia not being here for too long. Can't you understand why I'd want her back with me when it's so close to Christmas? I'd made plans…'

'I'm sorry about that, but sometimes whether we like it or not plans are hostage to change. The fact is that our daughter is safe with my mother in Copenhagen and you don't need to worry.' Sucking in a breath, Jake blew it out again onto the frosted air. He thumbed towards the bank of snow-covered cedars edging the road at the end of the drive behind him. 'There was a police roadblock on the way here, warning drivers not to go any further unless they absolutely had to. They only let me through because I told them you'd go crazy if I didn't make it to the house to let you know about Saskia. I only just made it—even in the SUV. I'd be mad to try and make it back to the airport tonight in these conditions.'

As if waking from a dream, Ailsa realised he looked half frozen standing there. Another few minutes and those sculpted lips would surely turn blue. As difficult as the prospect of spending time with her estranged husband promised to be, what could she do but invite him in, make him a hot drink and agree to give him a bed for the night?

'Well, you'd better come in, then.'

'Thanks for making me feel so welcome,' he answered sardonically as he stepped towards her.

His brittle reply cut her to the bone. Their divorce hadn't exactly been acrimonious, but coming less than a year after they'd suffered the terrible car accident that had robbed them of their longed-for second child, it hadn't been amicable either. Words had been flung…corrosive, bitter words that had eaten into their souls. But even now thinking of that horrendous time, of how their marriage had shockingly unraveled, was almost a blur to her because her senses had been so frozen by pain and sadness…like a delicate scallop sealed inside its shell after being relentlessly battered against the rocks.

Four long, hard years she'd lived without Jake. Saskia had been just five when they'd parted. Her daughter's poignant question, 'Why did Daddy leave, Mummy?' replayed itself over and over again in her mind most nights, disturbing her sleep and haunting her dreams…

'I didn't mean to be rude.' She grimaced apologetically. 'I'm just a little upset, that's all. Come in out of the cold and I'll get you a drink.'

He passed her into the hallway and the familiar woody scent of his expensive cologne arrowed straight into Ailsa's womb and made it contract. Inhaling a deep breath to steady herself, she hurriedly shut the door on the arctic weather outside.

The sixteenth-century beamed cottage that Jake had never been inside before was utterly charming, he mused as his senses soaked up the cosy ambience that greeted him. The lilac-painted walls of the narrow hallway were covered in a colourful array of delicate floral prints, intermingled with delightful framed photographs of Saskia as a baby, then a toddler, and a couple of more recent shots of her as a nine-year-old, already showing signs of the beauty she was becoming. And on the wall by the polished oak staircase the French long-case clock with its floral marquetry, its steady ticking peacefully punctuating the stillness...the stillness and peace that constantly seemed to elude *him*.

The snug little house felt so much more like a real home to Jake than the luxurious Westminster penthouse he rattled around in alone when he was in London, and even the smart townhouse he lived in when he was in Copenhagen. Only his mother's white-painted turn-of-the-century house just outside the city, which backed onto magical woodland, could match Ailsa's home for cosiness and charm.

When she had bought the cottage not long after they'd separated Jake had been seriously disgruntled by her refusal to let him purchase something far more spacious and grand for her and Saskia. *'I don't want something grand,'* she'd replied, her amber-coloured eyes making her look as though she despaired of him ever understanding. *'I want something that feels like home...'* The house in Primrose Hill that they'd bought when they'd married had no longer felt like home for either of them, Jake remembered, his heart heavy. *Not when the love they'd once so passionately shared had been ripped away by a cruel and senseless accident...*

'Give me your coat.'

His icy fingers thawing in the warmth that enveloped him, Jake did as she asked. As he handed over the damp wool coat he couldn't help letting his gaze linger on the golden light of her extraordinary eyes. He'd always been mesmerised by them, and it was no different now. She glanced away quickly, he noticed.

'I'll take off my shoes.' He did just that, and left them by the door. He'd already noticed that Ailsa's tiny feet were encased in black velvet slippers with a black and gold bow.

'Let's go into the front room. There's a wood-burner in there. You'll soon get warm.'

Fielding his turbulent emotions, Jake said nothing and followed her. His fingers itched to reach out and touch the long chestnut tresses that flowed down her slim back, he shoved his hand into his trouser pocket to stem the renegade urge.

The compact front room was a haven of warmth and comfort, with a substantial iron wood-burner at the centre throwing out its embracing heat, its funnel reaching high into the oak-beamed rafters of the roof. There were two red velvet couches laden with bright woollen throws and cushions, and the wooden pine floor was generously covered with a rich red and gold rug. Just one Victorian armchair was positioned by the fire. Two sets of pine shelves either side of the burner were packed with books, and in one corner—its roots embedded in a silver bucket—sat an abundant widespread Christmas tree waiting to be decorated. Jake's insides lurched guiltily.

'Sit down. I'll make us a hot drink…that is unless you'd prefer a brandy?'

'I don't touch alcohol any more. Coffee will be fine… thanks.' Now it was *his* turn to glance quickly away. But not before he'd glimpsed the slightly bewildered furrowing of Ailsa's flawless brow.

'Coffee it is, then.' She left the room.

Lowering his tall, fit frame onto a couch, Jake breathed out at last. For a while he watched the increasingly heavy snow tumbling from the skies outside the window, then fell into a daydream about his daughter playing on that sumptuous red and gold rug with her dolls. She'd be chatting away non-stop to them, he mused, her vivid imagination taking her far away from this world—a world that until she was five had promised a safe and secure day-to-day existence as she grew up, a comforting life that had abruptly changed beyond all recognition when her mother and father had separated.

He didn't realise Ailsa had returned until she stood in front of him, holding out a steaming mug of aromatic black coffee. Gratefully Jake took it. 'Just what the doctor ordered.' He tried for a smile but knew it was a poor effort.

'How is your mother coping since she lost your dad?'

He watched his pretty ex-wife walk across the room in that graceful, mesmerising way she had that made her look as if she glided. She'd always had that balletic quality about her, and the blue denim jeans she was wearing highlighted her slender thighs and tiny waist—especially with the broad leather belt she wore around her sweater. As she sat down on the other couch he tried to curtail his irrational disappointment that she'd chosen not to sit beside him. Her slender ringless fingers wrapped themselves around a mug of tea. From memory, Jake knew it was rare that Ailsa drank coffee. But he didn't dwell long on that. Inside he was reeling at the unexpected sight of the missing wedding band on her finger—another painful demonstration that their marriage had well and truly ended.

Clearing his throat, he garnered the defences that he'd fine-honed during the past four years without her. 'Outwardly she seems to be coping well,' he replied. 'Inwardly is another matter.' *He could have been talking about him-self...*

'Well, then, perhaps it's a good thing that Saskia stays with her for a bit longer. It's been, what...? Six months since your dad died?'

'About that.' Sipping the too-hot coffee, he grimaced as the beverage scalded his tongue. If it was Ailsa's aim to hold out an olive branch by not making a fuss about their daughter staying with her grandmother and spoiling her plans for the lead-up to Christmas, then he didn't intend to take it. He couldn't seem to help resenting the fact that she was clearly getting on with her life quite well without him.

'And how about you?' she persisted, low-voiced, leaning slightly forward, amber gaze concerned.

'What about me?'

'How are *you* coping with the loss of your dad?'

'I'm a busy man, with a worldwide property business to run...I don't have time to dwell on anything other than my work and my daughter.'

'You mean you don't have time to mourn your father? That can't be good.'

'Sometimes we all have to be pragmatic.' His spine stiffening, Jake put the ceramic mug down on a nearby side-table then flattened his palms over his knees. Ailsa had always wanted to get to the heart of things and it seemed that nothing had changed there. Except that he didn't feel like spilling his guts to her about his feelings any more... *been there, done that.* He had the bruises on his heart to prove it.

'I remember that you and he had your differences, and I just thought that his passing might be an opportunity for you to reflect on the good things about your relationship, that's all.'

'Like I said…I've been too busy. He's gone, and it's sad, but one of the things he taught me himself was to rise above my emotions and simply get on with whatever is in front of me. At the end of the day that's helped me cope with the "slings and arrows" of life far more than wallowing in my pain. If you don't agree with such a strategy then I'm sorry, but that's how it is.'

He sensed his temper and his unreasonableness rising. Privately he had nothing but contempt for such a tack. Leaving his father's death and his regret that they hadn't found a way to communicate more healthily aside, he reminded himself that he wasn't the only one in this one-time marriage who had been to the depths of hell and back. In the four years since their divorce Ailsa had grown noticeably thinner, and there were faint new lines around her sweetly shaped mouth. Perhaps she wasn't getting on with her life *that* well? He yearned to know how she was really coping. Saskia had told him that her mother worked long hours at her arts and crafts business, even at the weekends. *There was no need for her to work at all.* The divorce settlement he'd made for her was substantial, and that was the way he wanted it.

Jake frowned. 'Why are you working so hard?' he demanded, before he'd realised he intended to ask.

'What?'

'Saskia told me that you work day and night at this arts and crafts thing.'

'Arts and crafts *thing*?' She was immediately offended. 'I run a thriving local business that keeps me busy when I'm not doing the school run or tending to Saskia, and I love it. What did you expect me to do when we broke up, Jake? Sit around twiddling my thumbs? Or perhaps you expected me to spend my divorce settlement on a chic new wardrobe every season? Or the latest sports car? Or get interior designers in with pointless regularity to remodel the house?'

Wearily he rubbed his hand round his jaw. At the same time her words made him sit up straight. When he'd met her and married her he had never envisaged Ailsa as a businesswoman in the making. 'It's good to hear that your business is going well. And as regards the settlement, it's entirely up to you what you do with the money. As long as you take proper care of Saskia when she's with you—that's all I care about. I've noticed that you look tired, as well as the fact you've clearly lost weight…that's why I asked. I don't want you wearing yourself out when you don't have to.'

Her expression pained, Ailsa tightened her hands round her mug of tea. 'I'm not wearing myself out. I look tired because sometimes I don't sleep very well, that's all. It's a bit of a legacy from the accident, I'm afraid. But it's okay… I try and catch up with some rest whenever I can—even if it's during the day.'

If a heavyweight boxer had slammed his fist into his gut right then Jake couldn't have been more winded. It took him a few moments to get the words teeming in his brain to travel to his mouth. 'I told you years ago that you should get some help from the doctor to help you sleep better. Why haven't you?'

As she shook her head, her long chestnut hair glanced against the sides of her face. 'I've seen enough doctors to make me weary of ever seeing another one again. Besides…I don't want to take sleeping pills and walk round like a zombie. And unless the medical profession has found an infallible method for eradicating hurtful memories— because it's those that keep me awake at night—then I'll just have to get on with it. Isn't that what you advocate yourself?'

'Dear God!' Jake pushed to his feet. How was he supposed to endure the pain he heard in her voice? The pain he held himself responsible for?

Yes, they'd been hit by a drunk driver that dark, rainy night when their world had come to an end, but he still should have been able to do something to avert the accident. Sometimes at night, deep in the midst of troubled sleep, he still heard his wife's heartrending moans of pain and shock in the car beside him... He'd promised in their marriage vows to love and protect her always and that cruel December night he *hadn't*... He hadn't. He just thanked God that Saskia had been staying with his parents at the time and hadn't been in the car with them. It didn't bear thinking about that his child might have been hurt as badly as her mother.

He must be a masochist, he reflected. Why had he come here to tell Ailsa himself that Saskia was prolonging her stay with his mother? He could so easily have got his chauffeur Alain to do the deed. Wasn't that what he'd done for the past four years, so he wouldn't have to come face to face with the woman he'd once loved beyond imagining? Wasn't it a situation he'd willingly engineered so he wouldn't have to discuss the deeper issues that had wrenched them apart perhaps even more than the accident?

Sighing, he tunnelled his fingers through his hair. He was only staying the night while he was snowbound. As soon as the roads were passable again he would drive to the airport and return to Copenhagen. After spending a precious day or two with his daughter and mother he would get back to the palatial head offices of Larsen and Son, international property developers, and resume his work.

'I've got an overnight bag in the car. I brought it just in case. I'll go and bring it in.' When he reached the door he glanced back at the slim, silent woman sitting on the couch and shrugged his shoulders. 'Don't worry...I promise not to outstay my welcome. As soon as the roads are cleared I'll be on my way.' *Not waiting to hear her reply, Jake stepped out into the hallway.*

As hard as she bit down on her lip, Ailsa couldn't prevent her eyes from filling up with tears. 'Why?' she muttered forlornly. 'Why come here now and shake everything up again? I'm doing all right without you...I *am*!'

Frustrated by the unremitting sorrow that rose inside her whenever Jake or the accident were mentioned, let alone having him near, she stoically put aside any further thoughts on the matter and instead made her way up to the spare bedroom to put clean sheets on the bed for her ex-husband's unexpected overnight stay.

On the way there she pushed open her daughter's bedroom door and glanced in. The pretty pink walls were covered in posters, from the latest Barbie doll to instantly recognisable children's programme characters. But amongst them were two large posters of the latest male teen movie idol, and Ailsa shook her head in wonder and near disbelief that her daughter was growing up so fast...*too* fast, in her book. *Would it be easier if Saskia had both her parents taking care of her together instead of separately?*

In the time-honoured habit of caring parents everywhere, she wondered yet again if she was a good enough mother—if she was perhaps *failing* her child in some fundamental unconscious way? Was she wrong in wanting a career of her own? To stand on her own feet at last and not feel as if she was depending on her ex-husband? At the thought of Jake she wondered if she hadn't been utterly selfish in pushing him away emotionally *and* physically, and finally driving him into asking for a divorce. She should have talked to him more, but she hadn't. Relations between them had deteriorated so badly that they'd barely been able to look at each other, she remembered sadly.

Hearing the front door open, then slam shut again, she quickly crossed the landing to the spare room. The pretty double bed with its old-fashioned iron bedstead was strewn with all manner of knitting and materials from her craft business, and she scooped them up and quickly heaped them on top of the neat little writing desk in the corner. She wouldn't stop to sort them all out right now. Tomorrow she would venture out to the purpose-built heated office in the garden, where she created her designs and stored her materials, and she would store the colourful paraphernalia away properly. Right now she would concentrate on making the bed, so that Jake could bring up his overnight bag and unpack.

As she unfolded the pristine white sheets she'd retrieved from the airing cupboard Ailsa noticed that her hands were shaking. They might not be sharing a bed tonight, but it was a long time since she'd slept under the same roof as her ex-husband. Once upon a time they had been so very close—as if even an act of *God* couldn't tear them asunder. She'd often fallen asleep at night after they'd made love enfolded in his arms and woken the next morning in just the same position... *Her insides churned with grief and regret at what they had lost.* The haunting memories that Jake's appearance had brought to the surface again were so intense that it felt as if they might drown her.

'It's all right,' she muttered to herself. 'It's only for one night. Tomorrow he'll be gone again.' But as she glanced out of the window at the cascade of white flakes still steadily falling her stomach clenched anxiously. She might well be wrong about that...

* * *

Jake had gone upstairs to take a shower and get a change of clothes. Ailsa took the opportunity to retreat to the kitchen to mull over what to cook for dinner. She'd planned on having a simple pasta dish with a home-made sauce for Saskia and herself that night, but she was concerned that it wouldn't be enough to satisfy a healthy male specimen like Jake. He loved good food and the finer things in life, and was a surprisingly good cook himself. It was another reason why she was slightly nervous about cooking for him again. She was no domestic goddess, and during their marriage her husband had patiently tolerated her culinary attempts with great good humour—even if more often than not he had ended up suggesting they go out to eat at one of his favourite restaurants instead. Many times he'd suggested they hire a full-time chef or cook, but Ailsa had always insisted she loved to cook for her husband and daughter. At heart she was a traditionalist, and would have felt as if she'd somehow failed her family if she hadn't prepared their meals.

Having grown up in a children's home, it was inevitable that her greatest longing had always been to have a family of her own.

A heavy fall of snow rolled off the eaves outside the window and fell to the ground with a crash. Snapping out of her reverie, Ailsa reached for the kitchen telephone and listened intently for a dial-tone. *Nothing...* The lines were obviously still down. She was longing to hear Saskia's sweet voice and find out for herself if her little girl was happy with her grandmother in Copenhagen. Knowing how warm and loving Tilda Larsen was, she didn't doubt it, but she would have liked confirmation from Saskia herself.

Biting down on her lip, she reached for the apron behind the larder door and turned on the oven. She scrubbed and rinsed a couple of generous sized potatoes, pricked the skins with a fork and popped them in the oven on a baking tray. Then she retrieved some minced beef from the fridge, a couple of onions and some garlic, and arranged a chopping board on the counter. She would add the prepared pasta sauce to the ingredients in the frying pan, along with some kidney beans and rustle up a quick *chili con carne*, she decided. *At least it was a recipe she knew well, and therefore there was less chance of her having a disaster.*

'You look busy.'

The huskily male voice behind her almost made her jump out of her skin. Turning, Ailsa glanced into a sea of glittering iced blue, and her whole body suddenly felt dangerously weak. 'I'm—I'm just preparing our dinner.'

'Don't go to any trouble on my account.'

'It's no trouble. We've both got to eat, right?'

His gaze scanning the ingredients on the marble-topped counter, Jake shrugged. 'Need any help?'

'I'm fine, thanks.' Turning back to the job in hand, she picked up the waiting sharp knife to dice the onions. But it was hard to keep her hand perfectly steady when the image of Jake in a fitted wine-coloured sweater and tailored black trousers, his hair damply golden from his shower, kept impinging on her ability to think straight. 'I know when we were together my cooking wasn't great, but I've gotten better at it over the years and you might even be pleasantly surprised.'

The man standing behind her didn't immediately reply. When Ailsa heard him exhale a heavy sigh, she tensed anxiously.

'Why did you think your cooking wasn't great?'

'Well…you always seemed to end up suggesting we go

to a restaurant whenever I made anything. Perhaps that was a clue?'

Saying nothing, Jake moved up beside her and gently removed the ivory-handled knife from her hand. Laying it down on the chopping board, he turned her round to face him. 'I don't remember ever suggesting we go to a restaurant when you'd already spent hours in the kitchen cooking a meal. And when I suggested we eat out it was only ever to give you a break, so that you wouldn't stress over preparing something. You made some great food when we were together, Ailsa. You must have, because I'm still here…right?'

What special ingredient did he possess that made that crooked smile of his so heartbreaking? His eyes so penetratingly, flawlessly blue? Her breath hitched and her heart started to race…

CHAPTER TWO

IT PAINED Jake that Ailsa had harboured the belief all these years that he'd thought her cooking unpalatable. *Yes, he had on occasion smiled at her earnest efforts when they hadn't quite worked out, but he hoped he'd conveyed that he was appreciative too.* He'd eat burnt offerings every day if he could turn back the clock to the time when they were together, before the shattering event that had torn them apart.

He breathed out slowly. As he examined her thoughtful amber gaze a ripple of undeniable electricity hummed between them.

'Yes, you're still here,' she quietly agreed with a reticent smile.

'Battle-scarred, but still alive and kicking,' he added, joking.

Ailsa's smile fled, as did the beginning-to-melt look in her eyes. 'Don't joke about that,' she scolded. Her tone was softer as she looped some silky strands of hair behind her ear. 'Does it still bother you? The scar, I mean?'

His heart thudding—as it always did whenever his scar came under scrutiny—Jake mentally strengthened his defences, hammering in iron nails to hold them fast. 'Do you mean am I worried that it's spoiled my good looks?' he mocked. Spinning away from her, he jammed his hands into his pockets, but quickly turned back again before she had a chance to comment. 'It's been over four years since I acquired it. I've quite got used to it. I think it gives me a certain piratical appeal...don't you? At least, that's what women tell me'

'Women?'

'We've been divorced four years, Ailsa. Did you imagine I would stay celibate?'

'Don't!'

'Don't what?'

'Be cruel. I don't deserve that. When I asked you if your scar bothered you, I meant does it still give you pain?'

'The only pain I get from it is when I remember what caused it...*and* what we lost that day.'

She fell silent. But not before Jake glimpsed the anguish in her golden eyes.

'Well,' she said after a while, 'I'd better get on with the cooking or we won't have a meal tonight at all.' Clearly discomfited by what he'd confessed, Ailsa returned to the counter to continue dicing onions. 'Why don't you go and make yourself comfortable in the living room and just relax?'

'Maybe I'll do just that,' he murmured, glad of the opportunity to regroup his feelings and not blurt out anything else that might hurt her. Gratefully, he exited the room.

The charming dining room had terracotta walls, exposed beams on the ceiling, and a rustic oak floor. In the centre of the sturdy table—also oak—several different-sized white and scarlet candles burned, lending a warm and inviting glow to the room now that the day had turned seasonally dark. The window blinds were not yet pulled down, and outside snowflakes continued to float past the window in a never-ending stream. In the past, when they'd been married and in love, Jake might have considered the atmosphere intimate. But something told him it wasn't his ex-wife's intention to create such a potentially awkward impression. *She'd always lit candles at dinner, whatever the season.* She simply loved beauty in all its forms.

She'd once told him that the children's home she'd grown up in had been bare of beauty of any kind and her soul had longed for it. Quickly he jettisoned the poignant memory, but not before berating himself for not encouraging her to talk more about her childhood experiences when they'd been married.

Now, at her invitation, he drew out a carved wooden chair, then tried to relax as she briefly disappeared to get their food. When she returned he watched interestedly as she carefully placed the aromatic meal she'd prepared in front of him, noting how appealing she'd made it look on the plate. He hadn't realised how hungry he was until he'd scented the chilli, and he tucked into it with relish when Ailsa told him to, 'Go ahead and eat…don't wait for me.'

'What do you think?'

The slight suggestion of anxiety in her tone made his gut clench. Touching his napkin to his lips, Jake grinned in a bid to help dispel it. Sitting opposite him, her long hair turning almost copper in the light of the gently flickering candle flames, she was quite utterly bewitching. A little buzz of sensual heat vibrated through him. 'It's delicious. I can't begin to tell you how welcome it is after a long day's travelling,' he answered huskily.

'That's all right, then. Would you like some juice or some water?' She was already reaching her hand towards the two jugs positioned on the raffia place-mat between them.

Jake nodded. 'Water is fine…thanks.'

They seemed to have an unspoken agreement not to

talk during the meal. But then, just as he finished every last scrap of the chilli she had prepared, Ailsa took a deep breath and brought an end to the silence.

'Was it snowing in Copenhagen when you left?' she asked conversationally.

'We've had a few heavy snow showers over the past couple of days, but nothing like you've got here.'

'Saskia must be pleased, then. She loves the snow. She's been praying for a white Christmas.'

Leaning back in his chair, Jake met her gaze warily. 'I'm sorry I didn't bring her home today.'

Ailsa didn't reply straight away and reassure him that she was okay with it. Behind her soft amber glance he sensed deep disappointment, and perhaps some residue of anger too. He blew out a breath to release the tension that had started to gather force in the pit of his stomach.

'I know you don't want to hear it, but I had so many plans for Christmas. I even told my customers to get their orders in early because I was taking an extra week off before Christmas Day to spend some time with my daughter. I'm really sorry that your mother lost your father, Jake, but she's not the only one grieving.' She was fighting hard to contain her emotion, and her beautiful eyes misted with tears.

'Grieving?' he echoed, not understanding.

'Have you forgotten what day it is today?' Her steady gaze unflinching now, she curled her fingers into the pristine white napkin now lying crumpled by her plate. 'It's the anniversary of our baby's death…the day of the accident. That's why I needed Saskia home today. If she was here I'd be focusing all my attention on her and wouldn't let myself dwell on it so much.'

For the second time since setting eyes on Ailsa after so long Jake felt winded. Then a plethora of raw emotion gripped him mercilessly, almost making him want to crawl out of his own skin. An intense feeling of claustrophobia descended—just as if someone had shoved him inside a dark, windowless cell and then thrown away the key…

'I've never noted the date,' he admitted, his dry throat suddenly burning. 'Probably because I don't need some damned anniversary to remind me of what we lost that day!' Pushing to his feet, he crossed to the window to stare blindly out at the curtain of white still drifting relentlessly down from the heavens. Vaguely he registered the scrape of Ailsa's chair being pushed back behind him.

'We haven't talked about what happened in years…not since the divorce,' she said quietly.

'And you think now's the right time?' He spun round again, feeling like a pressure cooker about to blow. Ailsa was standing in front of him with her arms folded, her expression resolute. Yet he easily noted the giveaway tremor in her lower lip that revealed she was nervous too.

'I'm not saying I want to dwell on what happened just because it's the anniversary of Thomas's death, but I—'

'Don't call him that… Our son wasn't even born when he died!'

At the reminder that they'd given their baby a name, Jake felt his knees almost buckle. If he didn't think of him as having a name then he couldn't have been real, right? He couldn't have had an identity other than that of an unborn foetus in the womb. It was the only way he'd been able to cope with the tragedy all these years.

The delicate oval face before him, with its perfectly neat dark brows, looked faintly horrified. 'But we *did* give him a name, Jake…a name and a gravestone, remember? Before the snow got really bad yesterday I took a bouquet of lilac asters and white anemones to the graveyard where he's buried. I do it every year at this time.'

The graveyard that housed the tiny remains of his son was situated in the grounds of a picturesque Norman church tucked away behind a narrow street not far from the Westminster offices of Larsen and Son. But Jake hadn't visited it since the day of the funeral. *That had been a bitter winter's day, when icy winds had cleaved into his wounded face like hot knives, and it was a day that he wished he could blot from his memory for ever.*

Pressing his fingers into his temples, he drove them irritably back into his hair. 'And that helps, does it?'

'Yes, it does, as a matter of fact. I know I was only seven months pregnant when he died, but he deserves to be remembered, don't you think? Why do you seem so angry that I've brought the subject up? Did you really expect to stay here the night and not have me talk about it?'

Feeling utterly drained all of a sudden, as well as a million miles away from any remedy that could soothe the pain and distress he was experiencing at the memory of the longed-for son they'd lost so cruelly, Jake moved across to the dining room door that stood ajar.

'I'm sorry...but I really don't think there's any point in discussing it. What can it possibly achieve? You have to let it go, Ailsa. The past is finished—*over*. We're divorced, remember? We've made new lives for ourselves. Who would have thought the shy young girl I married would end up running her own business? That's quite an achievement after all that's happened. Not everything ended in disaster between us. We've still got our beautiful daughter to be thankful for. Let's leave it at that, shall we?'

'Yes, we have Saskia—and I count my blessings every day that we have. And, yes, I run my own business and I'm proud of it. But do you really believe that if we don't discuss it the shadow of that dreadful time we endured will magically go away? If it was so easy to just let it go

don't you think I would have done it by now? I thought
that the divorce would help bring some closure after our
baby's death—help us both put it behind us and eventually heal. But somehow it doesn't feel like it has. How can
it when I've lost half of my family and can't even hope for
more children in the future? The accident robbed me of
the chance. Perhaps because we're not together any more
it helps you to pretend that it never happened at all, Jake?
"Out of sight, out of mind", as they say?'

Ailsa was so near the truth that Jake stared at her. He
hadn't really wanted a divorce at all, but he had finally instigated it when the agony and the blame he'd imagined he
saw in his wife's eyes every day began to seriously disturb
him. *He just hadn't been able to deal with it.*

'How can I pretend it never happened, hmm? I only
have to look in the mirror every time I go to the bathroom
and see this damned scar on my face to know that it did!
Anyway...'

He swallowed down a gulp of air and his thundering
heartbeat gradually slowed. It gave him a chance to think
what to do next...to try to blot out the torturous memory
of Ailsa being so badly injured in the accident that she'd
slipped into unconsciousness long before the surgeons had
performed a ceasarean to try and save the baby. The head
surgeon had told Jake afterwards that her womb had been
irreparably damaged and their infant hadn't survived. It
was unlikely she'd ever be able to bear a child again.

'I've brought some work with me that I need to take a
look at before I turn in. My father's death has meant that
I've become CEO, and inevitably there's a raft of problems
to sort out. Thanks for dinner and the bed for the night.
The food was great. I'll see you in the morning.'

Even though his excuse was perfectly legitimate, there

was no escaping the fact that it made him feel like a despicable coward.

'If you need an extra blanket, you'll find a pile of them in the oak chest at the end of the bed.'

Ailsa's tone made her sound as if she was determined to rise above her disappointment at his reluctance to yet again deal with the past. He silently admired this new strength she'd acquired, and was moved to hear the compassion in her voice…compassion that he probably didn't deserve.

'Sleep well,' she added with a little half-smile. 'Don't sit up too late working, will you? You've had a long day's travelling and you must be tired.'

Obviously not expecting an answer to her remarks, she gracefully moved back to the table, then methodically started to clear away the detritus of their meal. Knowing already that his unexpected appearance had disturbed and upset her, Jake fleetingly reflected again that he should never have come here. *Then he would have avoided this agonising scene.* His throat locked tight with the guilt and regret that made him feel, and he swept from the room. In the prettily furnished bedroom he'd been allocated, he glanced despairingly over at the neat stack of paperwork he'd left on the hand-stitched patchwork quilt that covered the bed and angrily thumped his chest with a heartfelt groan…

Knitting at the fireside, as was her usual habit before retiring to bed—*she was always working on something beautiful and handmade for a customer*—Ailsa took comfort from the rhythmic click of her needles along with the crackle of fresh ash logs she'd added to the wood-burner. After that altercation with Jake earlier she was feeling distinctly *raw* inside—as though her very organs had been scraped with a blade. Already she'd resigned herself to another sleepless night. Sometimes she didn't vacate the high-backed Victorian armchair until the early hours of the morning. What was the point when all she did most nights if she went to bed early was toss and turn? Sleep was still the most elusive of visitors. It wasn't usually until around five a.m. that she'd fall into an exhausted slumber, then a couple of hours later she'd wake up again feeling drugged.

She often wondered how on earth she survived on such a relentlessly punishing lack of sleep and was able to take care of Saskia and work too. The human capacity to endure never ceased to amaze her.

But she was even more unsettled tonight by the fact that Jake was occupying the spare room upstairs. Seeing him again had been wonderful and dreadful all at the same time. *But the sight of him had always made her react strongly.* The deeply grooved scar on one side of his chiselled visage made him no less charismatic or handsome, she reflected. She was grief-stricken at the idea he believed that it did. And. yes…she privately admitted it *did* make him look rather piratical—although she hadn't wanted to hear that other women thought so too. It nearly killed her that he seemed to have forgotten the passionate love they'd shared and moved on. There was no such 'normal' pattern of existence for her. How could she even *look* at another man with the prospect of a relationship at the back of her mind after someone like Jake Larsen?

She'd been a trainee receptionist in the Larsen offices when they'd first met. Only nineteen, yet brimming with determination to better herself after her difficult start in life, she'd been so grateful for the chance of such a 'glamorous' job when she'd barely had any qualifications under her belt. But she'd been studying hard at her local adult education facility to remedy that. When Jake had walked through the revolving glass doors one day, wearing a single-breasted black cashmere coat over his suit, his lightly tanned skin and blond hair making him look like some kind of mythical hero from one of those magical folk tales that had at their roots the trials and travails of life and the story of how the handsome hero and beautiful heroine overcame them together, Ailsa almost forgot to breathe.

As he'd walked up to her and her colleague, her much more confident fellow employee had whispered under her breath, *'It's the boss's son...Jake Larsen. He's come over from Copenhagen.'* But even before her colleague had told Ailsa his identity her heart had already turned over inside her chest at the arresting sight of all that sculpted Viking beauty and the spine-tingling charisma that Jake exuded. She'd *never* been so fascinated by a man before. And especially not a man who was clearly light years out of her league, who wore the mantle of authority and power as though it was a natural component of his DNA. Yet he'd warmly introduced himself to her, the most junior and inexperienced of his staff, as though she were no less important than one of the firm's directors, she recalled. When he had followed up his welcome to her with a near-incandescent smile—a smile that had wiped every thought clean from her head—she'd found herself well and truly under his spell...

'Blast!' She dropped a stitch, patiently unravelled the multi-coloured wool, then cast on again. The logs in the burner hissed and spat and she glanced mournfully across at the beautiful Norwegian pine standing in the corner. It poignantly reminded her of a shy young girl at a party, waiting to be noticed by a boy and asked to dance... Once upon a time, in another life, Jake would have happily volunteered to help her dress the tree, singing lustily along to the carols playing in the background and teasingly increasing the volume of his voice when she protested he was singing out of tune.

It hurt that he wouldn't discuss the baby's death with her. Ailsa had hoped such a discussion would help them be a little easier around each other and truly be able to move on. They hadn't had a prayer of being able to do that after the accident and then leading up to their divorce, when they'd both been so wounded, hurt and angry, blaming each other for everything. She'd even hoped that such a mutually frank discussion might at last help her to sleep better at night.

'Oh, well...' Murmuring under her breath, she sighed softly. *When he leaves tomorrow I'll just carry on as normal. It's not all bad... I've still got Saskia. And the business is doing well...better than ever, in fact.*

She bit her lip, trying hard not to cry. Sniffing determinedly, she wiped her eyes and lifted her gaze to the tree again. Her daughter might not be around to share in the joy that decorating a Christmas tree could bring but it wouldn't stop Ailsa from taking on the task herself. After all, it was something she excelled at. She ran a very successful business designing and making beautiful things— everything from tree decorations to hand-knitted sweaters and patchwork quilts. Plus, she and Saskia had been collecting and making decorative odds and ends the whole year for this season.

Feeling her spirits lifting a little, she put her knitting away and instead of dozing in the armchair, as she normally did, for the first time in months she went upstairs to bed...

His hand fumbling for the clock beside the bed, Jake groaned when his sleep-fogged brain registered the time. Realising that he must have slept the sleep of the dead, he tried to fathom why. Like Ailsa, he had become a veritable insomniac over the years following the accident. Sitting up and arranging a plump pillow against the iron-bedstead to support his back, he was just in time to hear the radiator in the room click and hum into life. Breathing out deliberately heavily, he wasn't surprised to see the plume of steam that hit the icy air.

Was the house usually this perishingly cold in the morning? He couldn't help feeling a spurt of annoyance shoot through him at the thought that Ailsa could have chosen to live in much more luxurious surroundings, with underfloor heating and every available comfort. Instead she had stubbornly opted for this too isolated cottage. Charming as it was, it wasn't the home he wanted his daughter to grow up in...

Rubbing his hands briskly together to warm them, he diverted this disturbing line of thought by wondering how soon he could get a flight back to Copenhagen today. Mulling over the possibilities—or *not* as the case might be—he shoved aside the patchwork quilt that covered the silk-edged woollen blankets and strode over to the window. Lifting a corner of the heavily lined floral curtain, Jake stared out at the incredible scene that confronted him with a mixture of frustration, disappointment and sheer bewildering astonishment.

As far as the eye could see and beyond everything was deeply blanketed in brilliant diamond-white. And fierce gusts of wind were making the still falling snow swirl madly like dervishes. Unless he could sprout wings and fly there'd be no getting out of here today. In any case, all the planes at the airport would surely be grounded in such Siberian weather.

'Damn!'

He stood there in black silk pyjama bottoms, his

hard-muscled chest bare, and willed himself to come up with a plan. But even as he seriously considered phoning his helicopter pilot back in Copenhagen he remembered the lack of service yesterday for both landlines and mobiles in the area. The current extreme weather conditions didn't bode well for the service returning any time soon. The helicopter option was clearly off the agenda. As he bit back his increasing frustration, a tentative knock at the door made Jake's heart race.

'Jake, are you up and about yet? I was wondering if you'd like a cup of tea?'

Instead of answering, he crossed to the door and pulled it wide. Her dark hair flowing down over her shoulders, slightly mussed as if she'd had a restless night, Ailsa stood in front of him like some wide-eyed ingénue in a kimono-style red silk dressing gown. She barely looked out of her teens, let alone the mother of a nine-year-old. Disconcertingly, that old sense of fierce protectiveness that he'd always felt around her came flooding back.

'Never mind me. You look like you could do with a hot drink to warm *you* up,' he told her gruffly. 'Why doesn't your heating come on earlier? Have you seen the weather outside? It's freezing in here.'

'The boiler is on a timer. And, yes, I have seen the weather. I don't think the snow has let up all night. But it's not surprising you're cold, standing there with barely a stitch on!'

Jake couldn't prevent the grin that hijacked his lips. 'You know I don't sleep with much on. Or had you forgotten that?'

'You didn't say whether you wanted a cup of tea or not,' she persisted doggedly, clutching the sides of the silk dressing gown more closely together and concealing her face by letting her hair fall across it.

But not before Jake saw that she was blushing. He experienced a very male sense of satisfaction at that. It was good to know that he could still get a reaction from her, despite all the muddied water flowing under the bridge between them...

'I definitely wouldn't say no to a hot drink of some kind. But let me take a shower first and dress before I join you downstairs.'

'Okay.' The slim shoulders lifted, then fell again before she turned away. As Jake closed the door on Ailsa's retreating back, she swung round again. 'Shall I cook breakfast for you as well?'

He hesitated. Purely because he'd just noticed the smudged violet shadows beneath her eyes that clarified his belief that she probably hadn't slept. 'I don't want to put you to any trouble,' he said huskily.

A fleeting smile curved the pretty lips he'd so loved kissing—still *dreamed* of kissing from time to time, whenever he tortured himself with thinking back to what they'd had.

'It's no trouble.' She continued on her way down the landing and the gentle womanly sway of her hips made Jake's heart ache.

CHAPTER THREE

EMERGING from the living room, flustered and hot after making up the fire with some freshly cut applewood logs, Ailsa brushed her dusty hands down over her jeans and glanced up at the very same moment that Jake descended the staircase. No matter how many times she'd seen him... lived with him, loved him...it still gave her heart a jolt to be confronted with the sheer physicality of his presence. He was dressed much more casually this morning than yesterday, his long muscular legs encased in softly napped light blue denims, and he wore a white tee shirt beneath a black V-necked wool sweater. His sun-kissed hair looked as if it had been finger combed rather than brushed, and when he turned towards her and smiled his clear blue eyes were no less a magnet for her than they'd always been.

She didn't even notice the cruel scar on his cheek because her attention was so consumed by his gaze.

'I'll put the kettle on again and make some tea. I'm sorry if I'm a bit behind with the breakfast but I had to make up the fire. Did you sleep all right?'

'Like a baby,' he drawled. 'That's one hell of a comfortable bed.'

'When you consider that most people spend half their lifetime in bed, a comfortable one has got to be pretty essential, don't you think?' *Argh! She was babbling because she was suddenly inexplicably nervous around him.* And, however innocent, the last topic in the world she wanted to discuss with her charismatic ex-husband was bed!

When Jake merely grinned instead of commenting, as though he knew very well how uncomfortable she was, Ailsa quickly tore her glance away and headed down the hall to the kitchen. Her house guest followed her. She quickly washed her hands, then flicked on the switch to boil the kettle again. She was reaching for a couple of pottery mugs from the dresser when Jake pulled out a chair at the breakfast table and sat down. Knowing that his interested gaze trailed her every move, she grew more and more discomfited. Although she was tense and on edge in his company, she knew that if she turned round right then her ex wouldn't be displaying any such similar tension. When he *did* relax he turned it almost into an art form. His athletic body knew how to lounge to mouthwatering effect...even in a hard-backed kitchen chair.

Ailsa bit back a sigh. Deciding to bite the bullet, she made herself bring up the subject that had been at the forefront of her mind since waking that morning and seeing the breathtaking result of last night's heavy snowfall.

'If you were hoping to get to the airport today I don't think much of your chances.'

'Neither do I,' he agreed. The smooth skin between his brows puckered. 'Have you checked to see if there's a phone line yet?'

Ailsa grimaced. 'Yes, I have...it's still out, I'm afraid.'

'Damn!'

The harsh-voiced comment didn't do a lot for her confidence. *Had he come to dislike her so much that the thought of spending any more time than necessary in her company was abhorrent to him?*

'I feel just as frustrated that I can't talk to Saskia,' she murmured. Realising that the kettle had boiled, she swallowed down her hurt, then busied herself making the tea. She took Jake's over to him at the table. 'Help yourself to sugar. I'm going to get on with cooking your breakfast.'

'Are you going to join me?'

'I don't eat much in the morning. I'll probably just make myself a slice of toast.'

'Just toast? Is that all you have for breakfast?'

'Usually, yes.'

'Then it's no wonder you've lost weight.'

'Anything else you've noticed about me?' she asked, stung. It hardly made sense since they weren't together any more, Ailsa knew, but the notion that he might find her skinny and unattractive upset her. Yes, she'd always been on the slender side, but before the accident she'd had some nicely rounded curves too. Curves that he'd professed to *adore*. And when she'd been pregnant with Saskia, and then their son, he'd loved her womanly shape even more.

Did he spend his time adoring some other woman's curves these days?

Jake's steady, unwavering glance told her he was considering the question deeply. 'Yes. You're even more beautiful than I remember.'

'No, I'm not.' Her arms went protectively around her middle. 'Events have inevitably shaped me, and I'm very aware that I'm a little too thin and tired-looking. I'm twenty-eight, but sometimes I feel more like a hundred.'

'That's just crazy talk.'

'It's not that I even mind really.' She shrugged. 'As long as I have the energy to work and take care of Saskia, that's all that matters.'

Ailsa hadn't realised that he had risen to his feet until he stood in front of her, tipping up her chin to make her look at him. His eyes were such a searing sapphire-blue they were nearly the undoing of her. Had his lashes always been that long and lustrous? He was standing so close that surely he must hear the sound of her galloping heart?

'You might be tired, but you're not too thin and you certainly don't look old before your time. As a matter of fact I thought when I saw you yesterday how incredibly young you still are. Perhaps you were too young when I married you, hmm?'

Softly smoothing back her hair from her forehead, the palm that glanced against her skin was slightly rough edged, yet infinitely soft at the same time. *Like velvet.* Along with his deep, mellow voice, it almost lulled her into believing that everything that was wrong between them could be set right again.

Where had *that* dangerous notion sprung from? *The idea was as self-destructive as hoping for sanctuary in a burning house…*

As if coming out of a trance, Ailsa stepped back from Jake to cross her arms protectively over her chest, almost as if guarding her heart. 'Are you saying that you regret our marriage?'

He raised an eyebrow. 'I'm not saying that at all. Why do you always have to go on the defensive and believe the worst?'

Now *her* gaze was unwavering. 'Because some days it's hard to believe in anything good any more,' she told him honestly.

'It grieves me that you feel like that.' Sighing heavily, Jake narrowed his gaze. 'We had some good times when we were together, don't you remember?'

'We did… But then we made the painful mistake of believing we had a wonderful future in prospect…you, our children and I. Look what happened to that particular little fantasy.'

Why did she do this? Go for the jugular every time?
Hearing the despair in her voice made Jake feel as though
his heart was being slashed to ribbons again…just as his
hands had been in the accident, when he'd reached for
Ailsa to protect her from the splintering glass and jagged
metal that the drunken driver had recklessly and devastatingly reduced their car to, killing their beloved baby in
the process. He'd already had to bear the unbearable…how
long did the fates intend him to suffer?

In an agony of pain and frustration he squeezed his eyes
momentarily shut. When he opened them again Ailsa had
already moved back to the stove to cook breakfast. Staring at the glorious waterfall of long dark hair that waved
down her back, he wanted to step up behind her, pull her
too-slender form hard into his body and never let her go.
Instead he glanced out of the window in front of her to
see an even heavier curtain of snow descending from the
cobweb-grey skies.

'Is there to be no end to this godforsaken weather today?'

He made no attempt to disguise the anger and despondency in his tone, and Ailsa glanced round at him. 'I
know you can't wait to be gone, to be back in Copenhagen again…but you're going to be utterly miserable if you
can't accept the fact that right now you're stuck here for
a while. Just as I have to accept the fact that Saskia won't
be with me for another week.'

'Make me feel even worse than I do already, why don't
you? Don't you think I feel bad enough, showing up here
without her? My mother and she were so adamant they
wanted to be together for a little while longer, and I thought
why not? Where's the harm? I thought surely you'd understand for once, but instead you're regarding me like I've
committed the crime of the bloody century!'

'Jake, I—'

There was a loud hammering on the front door that made them both start.

'Who the hell is that?'

There was only one person it could be in this unbelievable weather, Ailsa realized. *And she knew his appearance probably wasn't going to help ease the current friction between her and Jake.* Wiping her hands down the front of the apron she wore, which was patterned with tiny red robins in honor of the season, she hurried out into the hall.

Stamping his feet on the doorstep, trying to shake off some of the frost and snow that caked his boots and fur-lined parka, was the handsome, dark-haired son of the farmer who was her closest neighbour.

'Good morning, Ailsa.'

'Linus, what are you doing here?'

'I've brought you some eggs, milk and bread to help tide you over until you can get to the shops again. Nothing can move out there except the tractor. Are you okay? I was worried about you and Saskia being here all on your own.'

'I'm absolutely fine, thanks—and Saskia's still with her grandmother in Copenhagen. It's very good of you to come and check up on us like this.'

'What are neighbours for?' A friendly grin split his lips, showing well-tended white teeth. 'Just a second and I'll go and grab those provisions.'

As she waited for him to return to the impressive red tractor that was steadily being drowned in even more layers of thick snow Ailsa clapped her hands together to warm them. The frosted air was literally like *ice*.

'Shall I take it through to the kitchen?' her visitor suggested, returning with a medium-sized cardboard container.

'Yes, please.' Forcing a smile to her lips, Ailsa sensed apprehension seep into the pit of her stomach at the thought that he was going to come face to face with her ex-husband.

There was nothing but casual friendship between her and the farmer's son—she'd never even remotely felt like advancing their association into anything more mean-ingful—but somehow, even though they'd been apart for a long time, she knew Jake would immediately jump to conclusions. The *wrong* conclusions… He'd always had a propensity to be jealous. But, although *he* had clearly entertained the possibility of another relationship, after that reference he'd made to women thinking he looked 'piratical', Ailsa *hadn't*. How could she *not* welcome in a friendly neighbour who had been so thoughtful? That was just plain bad manners in her book. The least she could do was make Linus a cup of tea to warm him up before send-ing him off on his journey home.

But as soon as they arrived in the kitchen Jake's aloof air easily conveyed his suspicion and even his annoyance at the presence of the other man. His glacial glance was colder than the icy weather outside as he silently surveyed the stranger who followed Ailsa in.

'Jake, this is my neighbour Linus—he's very kindly brought me some provisions from his farm. Linus, this is Jake Larsen…Saskia's father. He came to let me know that Saskia was staying with her grandmother a bit longer and now he's stranded here.' She subconsciously gnawed her lip at the realisation that Jake might well be annoyed that she'd given the other man a little *too* much information.

'I've heard a lot about you.' Linus frowned before quickly setting the box of provisions down on the table. He stole a brief glance at Ailsa before recovering his sur-prise and politely extending his hand towards the other man. 'From Saskia, I mean. She talks about you all the time.'

'Is that a fact?'

Although Jake paid deference to good manners and shook the other man's hand, the gesture was clearly reluctant. For a second all Ailsa could hear was the beating of her heart in tandem with the stolid ticking of the antique clock on the mantelpiece. Lightly touching Linus's arm, she made herself smile, as though everything was perfectly normal and her ex-husband *wasn't* wearing an expression that would repel even the most dogged comers.

'It is.' Her visitor's smile was awkward.

'Why don't you sit down, Linus, and I'll make you a nice cup of tea?'

He shrugged, clearly discomfited by Jake's frosty reception. 'That's kind of you, but I'd better not stay…there's still plenty to do on the farm before the daylight goes. But thanks for offering. Maybe I'll drop in again to see how you are in a day or two?'

'Are you sure you don't want a hot drink? It's freezing out there.'

'I'll be okay. I'm used to working in all weathers, and I've had a big breakfast this morning to help sustain me.'

'All right, then.' One eye on Jake, Ailsa clamped her teeth anxiously down on her bottom lip. 'Thanks so much for bringing those provisions. That was thoughtful. I owe you.'

'Don't be daft. It was my pleasure. To tell you the truth it was nice to have an excuse to drop round and see you. Sometimes work is relentless, and I don't get the time to visit as much as I'd like.'

His awkwardness had vanished, and now Linus's smile was broad. She was a little taken aback by it—especially

in front of Jake—but she privately owned to feeling pleasure too at being so warmly regarded.

His glance briefly moved across to her ex. 'It was good
to meet you,' he said.

'You too.'

The reply was uttered without expression, and Ailsa
thought it was just as well that Linus wasn't staying longer, because she definitely sensed that her brooding ex-
husband had hardly welcomed the idea.

'If we don't meet again I hope you have a safe journey
home.'

This time Jake said nothing at all. He simply looked at
the other man as if he wished he would disappear.

Linus smiled faintly at Ailsa, then turned and went out
into the hallway. When she returned to the kitchen, after
waving him goodbye, she clenched her fists down by her
sides and stared hard at Jake. There wasn't so much as an
ounce of remorse on his striking face for his distinct cool-
ness towards the other man, she saw. Her blood pumped
with indignation.

'Did you have to be so aloof? Linus is a good man. He
only came to check up on me and Saskia to make sure we
were all right. He even brought us some supplies because
I can't get to the shops.'

'Are you telling me that you're in need of another man
around these days to look out for you and my daughter?'

In sheer disbelief at what he was assuming, Ailsa
clenched her teeth. 'He's not "another man" in the way
that you're insinuating. For your information, Jake, I don't
need another man for anything! I can take perfectly good
care of myself. Linus is just a friend and neighbour.'

Rubbing his forehead, Jake momentarily glanced down
at the floor. When he lifted his gaze the crystalline blue
eyes glinted dangerously. 'You're telling me you can't see

that he wants to be much *more* than just a friend and neighbour?'

'What?'

'Perhaps things have progressed beyond friendship and
neighbourliness already?'

'We've had an occasional cup of tea and a chat together
and that's all. I've certainly never encouraged anything
more personal than that. And even if I had it's none of
your business who I spend my time with…not any more.
Did you forget that we're divorced?'

'No.' For a moment his expression bordered on tortured.
'I didn't forget.'

The annoyance and indignation that had threatened
to overwhelm Ailsa a few moments ago deflated like a
burst balloon. Now, instead of annoyance, the predomin-
ant feeling that coursed through her veins was compassion. They'd both been badly injured in the accident that
had killed their longed-for baby, and if that wasn't enough
they'd also endured the devastating end of their marriage.
On top of that, Jake had recently lost his father. He had to
be hurting.

*Was his anger towards her over the thought that she
might be seeing someone else a cover for that hurt?* More
than ever she realised they needed to talk. Somehow during this enforced stay of his at the cottage they had to find
a way to start resolving their shared agony from the past.

Her gaze came to rest on the sturdy cast iron frying pan
she'd left on the stove. 'I'll get on with cooking your breakfast. Do you want another cup of tea? That one's probably
gone cold by now.'

Returning to sit down again at the pine table, Jake pulled
the mug of tea that Ailsa had made earlier towards him
and took a sip. 'It's fine,' he murmured.

She was by his side in an instant, taking the mug from

his hands and cupping her hands round it to glean if the beverage was still sufficiently hot. 'It's practically cold. I'll make you another one. It's no trouble.'

'Why are you being so pleasant towards me when I've just upset you with my less than warm reception of your friend?' Disturbingly, Jake trapped her with his unflinching gaze.

'Is it going to help us if I'm *unpleasant*?' she asked reasonably.

A faint smile curved his lips. 'I guess not.'

'Then I'll get on with the breakfast.'

Opening the cardboard container Linus had left on the table, Ailsa retrieved a box of eggs. 'The eggs from the farm are amazing. They're new laid every day and better than anything I can get at the supermarket.'

'How lucky that you can get them from Linus.'

The comment was a bit more than lightly sarcastic, and she sensed the ground she thought they'd just gained slipping away. 'He *is* just a friend, you know. I wouldn't lie to you about that. I have Saskia's happiness to consider, as well as my own, and while she's still young I won't be in the market for a romantic relationship with anyone.' Her brow furrowing, she didn't draw away from Jake's interested glance. 'How about you? Are there any important new relationships in your life that I should know about?' Even as she asked the question her stomach lurched sickeningly in case he said yes.

To her relief, he shook his head. 'Like you, I don't intend to get seriously involved with anyone else until Saskia's grown. But nor have I resigned myself to some monastic existence either.' A muscle flexed in the plane of his cheek, just to the side his scar. 'I'm only human, and my basic human needs are no different to anyone else's.'

It took Ailsa a couple of seconds to find her voice after

that incendiary comment, because she was busy fielding the giant wave of hurt that washed over her at the idea of Jake having his sexual needs met by another woman... maybe even *more* than one woman. They'd been divorced for four years now, after all, and it was hardly the first time the thought had crossed her mind. Most times she quickly pushed it away. But she intimately knew her husband's needs in that department. *He had always been the most incredible lover.* That part of their marriage had fulfilled every dream of love and passion she had ever had *and then some...*

'What about *my* needs?' she asked, struggling to keep her voice level. 'Do I have the same freedom there as you do, Jake? Or don't you think I have such needs any more since the accident rendered me unable to bear children? Perhaps you think it's made me less of a woman?'

'Don't say that!' The flash of shock and dismay in his compelling blue eyes took Ailsa aback. 'Don't even *think* it, let alone say it. You're more a woman than any other female I know, and even though we're not together any more nothing will ever change that.' Getting to his feet he pushed back his chair. It was easy to detect he was breathing hard. Wordlessly, he lifted the box of eggs out of her hands and left it on the table. Then he slid his palm over her cheek, slid his thumb beneath her jaw to hold it steady. 'Saskia always says she has the most beautiful mama in the world, and she's right.'

'She would say that. She's biased.'

'Didn't you hear me?' His fingers tightened a little round her jaw...tightened *and* trembled. 'I said she's right.'

Twin desires of wanting him to say more, just to hear the smoky inflection in his voice at close quarters—a voice that could both comfort and seduce at the same time—and of longing to know what it would be like to feel his commanding lips on hers again swept through her. But Ailsa knew it wasn't wise to crave either of those things...not when she'd worked so hard to recover from the hurt and rejection that had come so close to breaking her. She'd lost her baby and then she'd lost Jake.

He might have instigated their divorce in a moment of black despair to finally escape the pit of despondency they had both sunk into, but Ailsa had readily concurred with it. The situation between them had become intolerable. They'd both needed breathing space. But even as she'd heard herself agree to legally ending their marriage she'd been utterly heartbroken at the prospect. *She didn't ever want to need him so much again.* She'd told herself over and over that Jake should be free to love again, to father a son with someone else. *Why hadn't he?*

Dangerously close to tears, she firmly removed his hand from her cheek and turned away. Then she turned back to collect the box of eggs from the table. 'Would you like one egg or two with your bacon?'

'You know what? I think I've lost my appetite.' The bleakness in his eyes moved through her like a knife.

'I'm not pushing you away, Jake. I just—' She breathed out a long slow breath, fighting to get her feelings under control. 'I just don't want to get hurt again, and neither do I want to hurt *you.* We've got no choice but to be together right now, so let's not spoil it, hmm? I'm totally open to talking about things, and maybe by the time it comes for you to leave we'll have resolved some of the issues that have bothered us so we can be more at peace with the choices we've made. What do you think?'

'Have you got a shovel?'

'What?' Not comprehending, Ailsa frowned.

Combing his fingers through his hair, Jake moved restlessly over to the window to glance outside. 'The path badly needs clearing. I'll go and see to it now…work up an appetite so that I can eat that breakfast you keep promising me.'

The unexpected humour in his tone gave her hope that he might at last be going to meet her halfway, so that they could talk freely about the past without blaming each other. 'Do you think it's worth doing right now? If it keeps on snowing it's going to be a thankless task. You'll have to go out and clear it all over again later.'

'If you were to step outside for any reason and take a fall, it's not something I want to have on my conscience when I leave. Just tell me where the shovel is, will you?'

Biting back *God forbid you should have me on your conscience,* Jake, and remembering she really *did* want to stop blaming him, Ailsa shrugged. 'Okay. Go out through the back door to the garden. You'll find one in the tool shed there,' she told him.

'Good. Can I put in my breakfast order? I think you'd better make it *two* eggs with my bacon. It could be hungry work,' he remarked wryly, crossing the stone-flagged floor to go outside.

CHAPTER FOUR

JAKE was honestly glad of the physical exercise as he put his back into clearing the snow laden path. The icy wind that stung his cheeks and made his eyes water—*just* occasionally—helped divert his mind from dwelling on Ailsa. It had been an almighty shock to the system to meet her neighbour Linus. If ever a man had a hopeful look in his eyes where a woman was concerned then Ailsa's farmer friend's look epitomised it. It wasn't that Jake was shocked that the man wanted Ailsa—what man in his right mind *wouldn't?*—it was *more* the fact that his beautiful ex-wife clearly had no idea that he desired her. That made her vulnerable. Sometimes she was just too naive for her own good.

It was funny that Saskia had never mentioned him to Jake—especially when he often asked her if her mother had any new friends. Clearly their young daughter didn't consider the farmer enough of a good friend to warrant talking about him to her father. Still…the man had no business casually dropping round, trying to sweeten Ailsa with his gifts—practical or otherwise.

Grim-faced, he stopped shovelling snow for a couple of minutes to stare up at the house. It was a compact, charming little cottage, chocolate-box perfect—especially as viewed now, dressed in its raiment of pristine white snow.

In truth, it was a million miles away from the luxurious houses and apartments his company sold across the globe to the rich and famous. But if they were happy here instead of somewhere more urban and expensive then what could he do? It had been clearly demonstrated to him by Ailsa over the years that she wanted as little interference and help from him as possible, and even though Jake didn't like it he couldn't blame her.

When that out-of-control car had hit theirs that stark December day he should have protected what was most precious to him against all the odds—even if it meant surrendering his own life to do so.

From deep within his soul an arrow of despair pierced him—so great that it almost made him double up with grief. Why had she told him that she visited their son's grave? *It wasn't as if he needed reminding that he hadn't survived.* His wife had been able to display her sorrow openly—to rant and rail at the heavens and shake with grief if she felt like it. In contrast, Jake had had to mourn his loss in silence, as well as appear as if he was handling it 'like a man'. In terms of being a great businessman, a good provider and a loyal husband to his wife, his father Jacob could definitely be regarded as a success, but when it came to expressing warmth and emotion he had been far too shut down for Jake to get close to. Consequently he had never truly felt he'd been loved by him.

Sometimes he cursed the pattern he had unconsciously adopted from the man who had raised him. To keep his emotions inside...not to show that his heart was breaking when he was hurt and to pretend that everything was okay.

Ailsa and he had lost so much. She believed they should talk. Did she really think they could overcome the tragedies that in the end had defined their once passionate union by merely *talking*? Jake's learned proclivity of keeping his feelings to himself was so ingrained that maybe it was too late to try and get past it?

Tasting salt on his tongue, he realised the tears that had been burning the backs of his eyes had tracked down his face. Furiously wiping them away—almost appalled at the emotional display that no one else was witness to anyway—he began shovelling the mound of snow on the path with extra zeal.

'Would you like some more bacon?'

'Are you kidding me? If I eat another bite I won't be fit for anything.'

'Are you sure?'

'Sure. Why don't you come and sit down for a minute?'

Jake's invitation was like being tempted with her favourite Swiss chocolate after Ailsa had vowed to give up the indulgence for good...

A silent war of attrition was already taking place inside her when his compelling glance mercilessly captured hers, and she sensed her defences pathetically crumble. 'Just for a minute, then.'

Carrying her toast and cup of tea across to the table, she sat down opposite him, her back to the large cream dresser that was laden with a colourful assortment of porcelain collectables. Outside the snowfall was gathering momentum but inside the house it was warm, snug and cosy—much more conducive to a little conversation than tearing around doing housework.

'I'm honoured.' His reply was gently mocking.

'Thanks for clearing the path, but I'm afraid it won't be long before it needs doing again. Not that I'm saying you should go out and do it,' she added quickly, her face growing hot.

'Anything physical is infinitely preferable to doing paperwork or gazing at a computer screen.'

Determinedly shoving aside the taunting images his smoky-voiced remark conjured up in her head, Ailsa smiled awkwardly and took a bite of her toast.

'You still enjoy doing crafts?' Cupping his hands round the cup of coffee she'd made him, Jake bestowed upon her the charming, slightly crooked smile that she'd always found so appealing, 'I guess that's a stupid question, considering you've turned it into a business,' he added.

'I do enjoy it...very much. It's only a small enterprise, but it's growing bit by bit. Some nice compliments from customers have helped. They're very loyal, and they tell their friends about me. Advertising online has boosted interest too. I was recently asked to do an interview for one of the top homes and interiors magazines.'

'Well done. That must mean a lot to you.'

'It does.' She lightly pursed her lips. 'When I think of where I came from it's a bit of a miracle, to be frank. I never thought I'd manage to accomplish anything worthwhile...at least in terms of a career.'

'Why would you believe that?'

'The conditions of my childhood, I suppose. Knowing that I was abandoned as a baby didn't exactly help. I've never quite been able to shake off the feeling that I was unwanted...therefore not good enough.'

'You've never told me that before.'

Feeling hot, and ill at ease because she'd unwittingly raised the topic, Ailsa nonetheless forced herself to meet the sudden intensity of Jake's examining stare. 'You never really asked about my childhood. I sensed it made you slightly uncomfortable—the fact that I came from a world so at odds with your own, I mean. That's why I never talked to you about it.'

Linking his hands together, he shook his head as if in surprise and disbelief. 'I'm sorry…sorry I didn't discuss such an important aspect of who you are and ended up having you believe I was uncomfortable with it. And I guess most of all I'm upset at the idea you thought you weren't good enough. I always knew how capable you were, Ailsa…how talented. Instead of just keeping it to myself I should have told you.'

There was a glow inside her at his words. But, even more than for what he'd said, she was just so glad that they were really talking at last…*connecting*. 'Anyway, I'm doing my best not to feel not good enough any more. Starting the business has really helped me in that department. It's also given me a boost to know that I can earn a reasonable income from my endeavours.'

Jake's scowl denoted that he didn't appreciate her answer. 'You're not short of money, and you don't have to depend solely on what you can earn for yourself.'

Hurt that he didn't appear to understand, Ailsa suddenly lost her appetite for even the single slice of toast she had made. 'I know you left me well provided for, Jake—and don't think I don't appreciate it. But it's important for me to know that I can support myself. I use the money you gave me for anything Saskia needs, but when and where I can I like to rely on my own income. Is it so hard for you to comprehend that I like being independent?'

'You were married to me once, and the money that was settled on you in the divorce is rightfully yours. Doesn't what most people would regard as a fortune make you independent enough?'

'I…' Feeling suddenly choked, Ailsa couldn't speak. Jake couldn't see that it wasn't the money *or* the amount that was important. It was what it represented to her…the death of their beloved baby and the end of their marriage.

At least the money she earned independently for herself came with no such painful or onerous baggage.

'Does that farmer friend of yours know that you're a wealthy woman?'

Her eyes widened. 'What are you suggesting? You think he only calls round because I've got money? Thanks, Jake. You really know how to make a girl feel special!'

Snatching up her plate, she shoved back her chair and strode away. She was leaning against the granite worktop, trying desperately to calm down, when Jake set down his coffee and came to stand in front of her.

'I didn't mean to suggest he only likes you because you have money. I just want you to be careful, that's all. I wouldn't want you taken advantage of. Sometimes you're too trusting for your own good.'

'And if I am why should you care?'

'Do you have to ask?'

'Is it because I'm the mother of your child? That's the only reason I can think of that you would care a jot about me.'

He actually *flinched*…just as though Ailsa had physically attacked him. Why, just then, did the scar on his face move her more deeply and terribly than it had ever done before? Before she'd realised, she had lifted her hand to gently trace its raised edge with her fingertips.

'Don't!'

She ignored the steely command and spread out her palm to cover his entire cheek. The bristles round his jaw made his skin feel like roughened velvet. 'I'm sorry I hurt you with what I said,' she told him softly.

Firmly circling her wrist, just as she had feared he would, Jake lifted her hand away.

'And I'm sorry that you really believe I couldn't give a damn about you. It's not true…'

As Ailsa's heart started to pound with regret and sorrow at the cruel events that had driven them apart, she found herself impelled hard against his seductive iron strength, her senses drowned by his compelling male warmth and deluged by memory, hurt and desire.

It was *desire* that took precedence. It touched her blood with fire, mercilessly scorching through her veins as he hungrily, without finesse, took possession of her lips. *The most disturbing thing of all was that she didn't try to stop him.* Just one taste of him was enough to remind her of what she had missed…what she had *pined* for when he'd left. Jake was like an opiate she still craved, even though she knew renewing such an addiction was a road that could only lead to further pain.

As his lips and tongue stoked the passion already consuming her his hands moved through her hair and then down her body, where they settled round her hips, hungrily bringing her closer. His belt buckle bit into Ailsa's belly even as she registered the steel-like evidence of his desire pressing against her. But even as her pelvis softened and the tips of her breasts surged against her bra beneath the sweater she wore shock rippled through her. She realised exactly what she was inviting…the *madness* and soul-destroying stupidity of such an act. Did she really believe that such reckless behaviour could fix anything? She was delusional if she did.

Breaking off the kiss, she wiped her hand across her still throbbing lips, breathing hard. 'This isn't a good idea, Jake.'

'It feels like a very good idea to me.' The grin that accompanied his smoky voice made her legs feel dangerously weak.

'Well, it's not. Do you really think succumbing to a

steamy grope in the kitchen will help us resolve all the problems of the past?'

He looked appalled. Then he looked angry. 'That sounds disturbingly cold. You might not need some human warmth from time to time, but *I* do—and I'm not ashamed of it either. And actually I wasn't thinking that what just happened between us might help us. I simply got lost in the moment. Once upon a time you liked that about me...my spontaneity, I mean. I'm going up to my room to do some work. I would tell you to call me if you need anything, but as I very much doubt you would forget I even mentioned it.'

At the door he briefly turned back, blue eyes mocking. 'On second thought, perhaps you'd prefer to call on your farmer friend? You certainly don't seem to mind accepting help or gifts from *him*!'

Shaken by the hurt that had deluged her at Jake's sardonic parting shot in the kitchen, Ailsa stood blankly in front of the pine tree in the living room, wondering how on earth she would even summon the energy never mind the *enthusiasm* to decorate it. Inside she was quietly devastated that Jake believed she didn't need or desire human warmth like he did. If he had known how much she'd loved the feel of his strong arms around her just now... If he had guessed how much being held by him and kissed by him felt like coming home...

He might think that she was more amenable to receiving Linus's help than his, but the other man didn't have a hope of ever getting a warm response in that way from her because she didn't *desire* him. *Not the way she desired Jake.*

Fighting back her tears at their sorrow-ravaged relationship, she moved across to the wood burner to add another applewood log. After stoking the simmering flame that licked round the previous incumbent, she carefully closed the small glass doors as a flash of electric blue heralded the fire fiercely taking hold again. *Christmas was traditionally a time for families,* she thought achingly, missing her daughter afresh. What would Saskia think if she could see her mother now, hesitating over decorating the Christmas tree with all the trinkets and baubles they had had such fun making together? *Come on, Mum,* she'd say, *It's nearly Christmas! Don't be sad...*

Spurred on by the idea of not disappointing her child, Ailsa hesitated no more. Her darling girl would return home to a Christmas tree *beyond* wonderful, she vowed.

At the back door that led onto the garden she braced herself to face the still swirling snow, pulled on her boots, coat and hat, then determinedly negotiated her way down the thickly frosted path to the purpose-built shed that housed her craftwork. Bringing back the large box of decorations she'd stored there, along with two generous strings of white lights, Ailsa quickly disposed of her outdoor clothing, then returned to the living room with her container of goodies in tow. Along with the delicious heat from the fire, the scent of warm apple immediately suffused her senses as she entered. It definitely made the atmosphere feel Christmassy.

Stowing the box of decorations by the tree, she crossed to the discreetly placed music centre on one of the bookshelves to switch on the CD that was already in there. As an orchestral rendition of 'Silent Night' filled the air, accompanied by a cathedral choir, she breathed a satisfied sigh and then returned to the elegant Norwegian Pine to start decorating...

Sitting on the bed with his arms around his knees, Jake

couldn't summon the slightest interest in working. The urgent mail his secretary had handed to him before he'd left Copenhagen would just have to wait. Right then he didn't care about the consequences.

He turned very still when he heard the notes of his favourite Christmas carol drift up the stairs. Positioning his arm behind his head, he lay back against the stack of plumped up pillows. The poignant music invited him to turn to more peaceful contemplation, but it wasn't easy. He'd been so angry with Ailsa just now, for all but pushing him away and rejecting him, that he'd allowed his hurt to consume him. *Steamy grope indeed!* He hadn't intended to kiss her, but the feelings that had been building inside him ever since he saw her yesterday morning had been growing more and more difficult to contain. Like a dam about to burst.

The kiss he'd stolen had been inevitable, the gesture totally spontaneous…spontaneous and *wonderful*. Even now Jake's body was in a heightened state of painful readiness to make love to her. For a long time after they'd parted his clothes had smelled of Ailsa. It had been a slow, sweet torture to scent her body and not be able to reach out and touch her. Every day had been an agony to him because he couldn't be with her… No other woman since had even come *close* to making him feel like she did. *So much for peaceful contemplation…*

Groaning, he turned over on his side and for a long while just watched the glittering white flakes drifting down outside the window. Then long-held fatigue—both physical and psychological—finally got the better of him and he fell asleep…

The third CD of carols had almost come to an end when Ailsa stepped back to take a proper look at her handiwork.

The handmade decorations that she and Saskia had been creating throughout the year looked a treat. At last the tree was dressed. Along with the glittering coloured baubles and bells, the twinkling white lights gave it the essential magical finish. As soon as daylight started to fade the full, enchanting effect would be apparent.

More than pleased with her efforts, she hummed along to the final track on the CD. It was 'In the Bleak Midwinter'. Not exactly the most uplifting of carols, but she loved it nonetheless. The head carer at the children's home she'd grown up in had always teased her that it was probably the Irish predilection for tragedy in her blood that made her love it so.

The only thing Ailsa knew about her mother was that she had been just sixteen when she gave birth to her and was Irish. Years later, when she'd tried to trace her whereabouts, all she had got was several dead-ends. Many times during her marriage to Jake he had suggested they hire a first-class detective to try and find her, but Ailsa had always declined. After trying to locate her for a while and having no luck she'd decided it wouldn't help her to dwell on the woman who was her mother. It was enough to know that she'd been abandoned—ergo *unwanted*. If her mother had wanted to find her then she would surely have tried years ago, she'd told Jake. *The truth was Ailsa was scared to find her in case she was rejected all over again.* She couldn't have borne that.

Shaking off the unhappy reflection, she started to gather up the odds and ends she hadn't used and began piling them neatly back into the cardboard container.

'Personally I much prefer "The Holly and the Ivy" or "Silent Night". This one is too much like its title…*bleak*.'

Her back to him as she stood up with the box in her arms, Ailsa jolted at the sound of Jake's voice coming from the doorway behind her. She swung round. The first thing she noticed was that his hair was more than a little bit awry, making him appear as if he'd just got out of bed. The second thing she realised was that his compelling deep voice was friendly—as if he wanted to make amends for his earlier irritation with her. Her heart skipped a beat at the mere idea.

'I was playing "Silent Night" earlier,' she replied.

'I know. I heard it. It sent me to sleep.'

'You must have needed the rest. Do you like the tree?'

He studied it for a few moments then smiled...*warmly.* 'It's magnificent. I wish Saskia was here to see it.'

As soon as the words were out of his mouth there was something in his expression that suggested he regretted them. Ailsa wondered if it was because he feared an emotional backlash. But for once, instead of allowing her emotions to get the better of her, she made herself smile.

'She'll see it when she gets home on Christmas Eve. Besides, I'm sure your mother will make her own tree equally if not more beautiful.'

'You're right—she will. If only because her granddaughter is there.'

'It's going to be tough for her...her first Christmas without your dad.'

Jake came right into the room. 'For sure,' he agreed readily, his blue eyes far away for a moment. 'But having Saskia there until the day before will make all the difference.'

Ailsa's disappointment and hurt that he hadn't brought Saskia home when he'd said he would dissipated. She almost couldn't bear the thought of the warm and gracious Tilda Larsen being on her own at Christmas without the man she'd loved since she was a girl beside her, and suddenly she was genuinely glad that her daughter was with her grandmother.

'Are you going to be with your mum on Christmas Day?' she asked.

'That's the plan—if this arctic weather ever clears.'

The box in her arms started to get a little heavy, and she put it down on the rug in front of her. Just as she was about to straighten up again she caught a glimpse of some spangled gold material. Reaching inside the colourful contents of the box, she retrieved the small figure of an angel that Saskia had lovingly made a dress for. A flood of warmth suffusing her chest, she smilingly held it up so that Jake could see it.

'The fairy that goes on the top of the tree... I know you only have a star in Denmark, but here we always have a fairy. Saskia spent ages choosing the material to make her dress with. It's a bit ostentatious, I know—but, hey...it's Christmas.'

'Do you think our little girl has pretensions of grandeur?' Jake suggested wryly.

Smiling fondly in agreement, Ailsa shrugged. 'She's a "girly" girl... She loves dressing up and adores anything pretty. Not like me as a child at all. I was a real tomboy—never happier than when I was dressed in jeans and tee shirt and covered in mud and dirt from the bottom of the garden, where I'd usually be found closely studying the population of worms.'

'And after you'd studied them...what did you do?'

'I took them back into the house to show everyone, of course!'

'You must have been a real handful for those who raised you.'

'The carers at the home, you mean? I certainly can't have been easy for them. I was never a "sit in the corner" type of child. I was always into something I shouldn't have been…a real rebel. I got a prospective adoption placement once, but I kept running away. The people who wanted to adopt me were good and kind, but by then I was so used to the home that I kept trying to break out of the house… even at night. Eventually they decided they simply couldn't handle a girl who rejected every bit of love they tried to give her.'

Saying nothing, Jake rubbed his hand over his chest.

Twisting a long silken strand of chestnut hair round her finger, Ailsa allowed her gaze to fall into his. *It was like diving into a bottomless blue lake.* 'That's probably why it wasn't easy to find anybody else to adopt me. I was a regular tearaway, by all accounts—not the sweet, malleable little girl everybody wanted me to be.'

'No doubt you had a lot of anger inside… It's understandable under the circumstances.'

'Who knows? It's in the past, isn't it?'

'Yes,' Jake agreed soberly. 'It's in the past. Do you want me to put that fairy on the top of the tree?'

'Would you?'

He was tall enough not to need a chair to stand on, and as he reached up to position the bright little figure on the central branch his sweater and tee shirt rode up his muscle-ridged torso. Ailsa gawked. He'd always taken care of himself, but he looked even leaner and fitter than before. She almost had to bite back a groan. His taste still lingered on her lips, in her mouth and on her tongue… The memory of their passionate kiss taunted her. Now her whole body was suddenly taken over by a deep carnal ache.

As Jake turned round again she strove hard to keep her expression neutral. 'That's great,' she told him. 'Just perfect. Saskia's going to love it.'

'Anything else you'd like me to do to help add to the festive atmosphere?'

'No.' She gritted her teeth and smiled. 'I don't think so.'

'What about stringing some lights up in front of the house? We always used to do that...remember?'

The memory was so bittersweet that tears immediately sprang to her eyes. Seeking refuge from his knowing glance, she gathered up the box of discarded decorations and moved to the door. Realising she was starting to distance herself from him again, she stopped to glance back over her shoulder. 'I remember. But it's freezing out there. Do you really want to go outside and do that?'

'I think it would be a nice welcome home for Saskia... don't you?'

That was enough to make Ailsa believe it was a good idea—a *very* good idea. When they'd been married they could easily have hired professional interior designers or decorators to make the house look stunningly festive, but each year, when the most magical season of all had come round, Jake had always insisted on stringing the lights outside the house himself.

'I'll go outside to my workroom and get some extra lights, then,' she told him.

'No, you stay here. Tell me where they are and I'll go get them.'

Her arms were still around the cardboard container, and her heart started to bump hard when Jake came to stand in front of her, smiling down with that ever so slightly crooked smile of his... It affected her so much that somehow she lost her grip on the box and it dropped to the floor, its contents spilling in a kaleidoscope of colours at her feet.

'I'm so clumsy!' she exclaimed, dismayed, instantly dropping down to her haunches to pick them up.

'Don't say that. You're not clumsy at all.' Helping her gently but firmly to her feet, Jake's hands were like a burning brand round the tops of her arms, and Ailsa was so captivated by his nearness, along with the blazing need she saw reflected in his brilliant blue eyes, that she was powerless to free herself...

CHAPTER FIVE

'YOU'RE beautiful and graceful.'

It was almost too hard for her to hear a compliment from him when they had seemed to be at war for so long. 'Don't say such nice things to me.'

'Why not, in God's name?' Looking perturbed that her amber eyes were awash with tears, Jake slid his hand beneath her jaw.

'Because if you say nice things then I can't stay mad at you,' Ailsa whispered back brokenly.

Almost unconsciously she'd been leaning towards him, and she didn't know or care right then who made the first inflammatory move but as soon as their lips met she knew she was lost…swept up in a maelstrom that she didn't have a prayer of resisting. Allowing the power of it to suck her under, she didn't protest when Jake held her face so that he could plunder and ravish as she ached for him to do. There was no doubt in her mind about letting desire have its way. She supped and drank him in with equally passionate ardour, hardly noticing that his beard-roughened jaw scraped her skin and would probably leave it feeling tender. Winding her arms round his lean, hard middle, she secretly thrilled at his indomitable male strength…the rock-solid physicality of him, the rugged warmth and scent that made her want to jump right inside him. It was, perhaps, the aspect of his presence that she'd missed the most.

It was actually Jake who regained his sanity first. With his hands still cupping her face he lifted his lips away from hers, his head making a rueful motion. 'You know where this is going to end if we don't call a halt to it right now, don't you? Are you ready for that, Ailsa? Is that what you want?'

She hadn't wanted him to give her a choice. If he had just continued kissing her until her lips were numb and she was too weak with desire to stand then she would have definitely succumbed to being seduced by him. But Jake *had* given her a choice, and now that sanity had prevailed she was moved to act on it.

'I'm sorry,' she murmured. Her face burned with guilt and embarrassment as she shakily stepped out of his embrace. 'Call it a weak moment.'

'What we had between us was never weak or half-hearted, baby. It was always like a lightning storm. It seems that some things haven't changed as much as we thought they had.'

'I can't deny it.' Regret was like a heavy blanket smothering her—regret that Jake had stopped kissing her and regret that an accident had destroyed all their hopes and dreams and torn them apart. Ailsa wished she knew a way to throw off that smothering blanket for ever. Unfortunately she didn't. 'But I know that if we give in to it,' she continued across the ache in her throat, 'it might satisfy a momentary urge but it's not going to mend anything. How can it? We've built separate lives Jake. They may not be perfect, but living apart has kept us from blaming each other for what happened and being angry all the time. Towards the end we were so bad to each other, and I really regret that. We added to our suffering by making each other feel guilty. At least we both get a little peace now, and so does our daughter.'

'Peace? Is that what you call it?' His mouth twisting with derision, Jake muttered a curse. 'The memory of that accident is like being hunted day and night by a pack of rabid wolves. No matter what I do, no matter where I go, I'm never free of the darkness it brings. I'm glad that you feel peace sometimes, Ailsa. I really am. But I can't say that I ever do. I was going to string the lights. I'll go and get them.'

He was out through the door before Ailsa could call him back…

Adding another sweet-smelling applewood log to the wood-burner, Ailsa sat back on her heels. Glancing up at the clock on the mantelpiece, she noted that Jake had been outside stringing lights in freezing temperatures for at least a couple of hours now. Earlier, remembering that he didn't touch alcohol these days, Ailsa had taken him a warming mug of non-alcoholic mulled wine. He'd reached down from the ladder he'd rested against the cottage's sturdy stone walls, murmured 'thanks', then climbed back up the ladder without so much as a backward glance.

The chasm of hurt and tension between them was like an icy splinter embedded in her heart. By the time the weather let up sufficiently for him to be able to travel home would that chasm have grown even wider? Swallowing down her concern that it might, and worrying about the implications for their daughter, she impatiently rose to her feet and headed for the kitchen. Somehow they had to make peace with each other—for Saskia's sake if not their own.

As she entered, the back door opened and Jake put his head round the door. 'I've finished. Do you want to come outside and take a look?'

As his wary glance scanned her, she was struck near-speechless by the dazzling glitter of his piercing blue eyes. It was so easy to fall into a trance looking into them sometimes.

'Give me a minute. I'll just get my coat.'

At the front of the house sparkling white lights dropped in concentric arcs just like a stunning diamond necklace. Even though she was good at crafts and had an eye for design Ailsa knew she could never have come up with anything nearly as beautiful or exquisitely elegant. She was touched that Jake had taken so much time and trouble—and in weather that would have driven most people to hurry back indoors just as soon as they could.

Turning round to study him, she saw how the icy wind had seared his cheeks red raw and felt a leap of concern. 'You've done a wonderful job. Saskia will be over the moon when she sees it.'

'They'll look even better when we switch them on later.'

'They will. But you should come inside now and get warm. You look half frozen. Are you hungry? I'll make some sandwiches and coffee.'

'That sounds great.'

Shucking off his boots on the mat inside the door, Jake hung up his fur-lined jacket and made a cursory attempt to dislodge some of the ice and snow that clung to it. Shivering hard, he clapped his freezing hands together to try and restore his circulation. It was hard to remember when he had last felt so deathly cold. Fixing the lights had been intricate work, and gloves would have rendered the task impossible so he hadn't bothered with them. But it had been worth enduring the stinging snow and icy wind to hear the pleasure in Ailsa's voice at what he had done—to imagine his daughter's delight when she saw the sparkling display.

God, how he missed his little girl... All he wanted to do
at Christmas was watch her tear open her presents and then
sit with her and hug her tight. Sadly, that wasn't going to
be possible, when she would be here in England with her
mother and he would be back in Copenhagen. Jake had
spent the last four Christmases alone. He'd even declined
the usual loving invitations from his mother to spend the
holiday with her and his father. The relationship between
the two men had become more and more strained due to
Jake's desire to bring new innovation into the company—
not just to stick to the traditional Larsen way of doing business. Instead of being pleased at his son's ideas, his father
had seen his efforts as a bid to somehow usurp him. It
seemed that no matter what he'd done Jake had never managed to gain the older man's approval. Spending Christmas
with his family would only have exacerbated his unease
and pain.

He sighed. It had become a tradition for Ailsa to have
Saskia with her over Christmas...especially on Christmas
Day...and because of his guilt about past wrongs he'd simply allowed the tradition to continue. But the truth was
he didn't want to be with anyone else but his child at that
time, and if he couldn't be with her then he would rather
be alone.

As he stepped into the warm and cosy kitchen, to find
Ailsa humming another familiar carol beneath her breath
as she stood at the counter slicing bread, he suddenly knew
that it wasn't just his daughter that he wanted to spend that
day with. Knowing the very *idea* would just exacerbate the
heartache he already endured daily, he quickly jettisoned
the thought to the furthermost corners of his mind.

'I'll make the coffee, shall I?'

'Could you?' She threw him an absent-minded smile
that all but cut him off at the knees. Even though he'd just

spent a freezing couple of hours outside, putting up the lights, his body still ached with the kind of heat that could spark a forest fire—to hold her close and make love to her again one last time...

'Jake? Are you okay?'

'Loaded question.' Grimacing, he moved towards the other end of the counter to switch on the kettle. 'Where do you keep the coffee?'

'I bought a new Colombian blend. Do you want to give it a try? It's in the white porcelain jar...the one from Denmark that your mother gave me our first Christmas together.'

Wincing at the bittersweet memory of his mother's gift, Jake lifted the lid on the aforementioned jar and appreciatively sniffed the coffee grounds contained inside. 'Smells good. Are you going to join me in a cup, or would you prefer your usual tea?'

'I'll have a cup of coffee with you. You can make it in the large cafetière, if you like.'

'Breaking routine, I see?'

As she paused in her careful spreading of butter on the bread, Ailsa's glance was prickly. 'I do occasionally enjoy a cup of coffee, you know. I don't always have tea. You make me sound very boring and predictable.'

Amused by her tetchy defence of her choice, Jake stretched his lips into a grin. 'I wasn't suggesting you were boring or predictable. That's not something I would ever accuse you of. In fact, your unpredictability definitely kept me on my toes during our marriage.'

'That sounds very much like I was unreliable. Anyway, *how* did it keep you on your toes?' Her amber gaze was both quizzical and slightly irritated.

'I didn't mean to suggest you were unreliable. I just meant that sometimes you said you were going to do one thing and then at the last minute you preferred to do something else. Do we have to go over the details?' Carefully he measured out two generous scoops of coffee into the cafetière. 'Isn't it enough that I was charmed by your maverick nature? I wasn't complaining about it.'

'That's all right, then.' With a sniff, she turned back to making their sandwiches.

He didn't know why, but on some level Jake was encouraged that Ailsa still minded what he thought of her. He might be grasping at straws, but right then he didn't care.

'Did you warm the pot before you put the grounds in?' Waving a vague hand, she cut the sandwiches into triangles, then arranged them on two daintily scalloped white plates and carried them across to the table.

Staring at the grounds he'd already scooped into the cafetière, Jake ruefully dropped his hands to his hips. 'No, I didn't.'

'Never mind. I don't always remember to do it either.' She flashed him a genuinely warm smile, and suddenly the winter inside him was supplanted by tantalising summer.

'Thank the Lord for that. I thought you were about to throw me out into the snow in disgust!' he returned jokingly.

'I would never do— Come and eat your sandwiches.' Colouring a little, and looking discomfited, she sat down at the table.

'I'll make the coffee first.'

When he finally sat down opposite Ailsa, Jake rested his elbows on the table and linked his hands, making no move to touch either the food or the coffee—not when he'd much rather contemplate the exquisite features in front of him that made his heart jump every time he gazed at them.

'You're miles away. What are you thinking about?'

She'd always used to ask him that, he remembered, and usually he'd have been thinking about *her...* How lovely she was, how lucky he was to have found her and married her, and how much he adored her. *It was a shame he hadn't spoken those thoughts out loud,* he thought now. *Especially when he'd since learned that she hadn't felt good enough.*

'I was thinking how much Saskia resembles you,' he said instead. It wasn't a lie. Sometimes his daughter's smile stole his breath because it reminded him of Ailsa so much...

'She has your amazing eyes,' she replied softly, following the comment up with a self-conscious shrug.

The warmth in Jake's belly increased tenfold. 'Blue eyes are ten a penny where I come from.'

'But there are many shades of blue...yours is particularly unusual. The colour is like the blue you get at dusk.'

Silence fell between them as their glances met and clung—magnetised by a longing that had somehow miraculously escaped untarnished from the ashes of the past. He hardly dared inhale a breath in case he somehow caused it to vanish.

'Shall I pour the coffee?'

Already lifting the cafetière, Ailsa deposited some into the two slim scarlet mugs Jake had brought to the table. He noticed that her hand shook slightly as it curled round the handle.

'I'm afraid I need some milk and sugar. I can't drink it without.' She rose up quickly from her chair, leaving the hauntingly rich and melancholy trail of her own particular fragrance behind.

His stomach clenched so tight that Jake covered the clutch of iron hard muscles with his hand in a bid to ease the ache.

'Has Saskia told you what she'd like from Father Christmas this year? I suppose we ought to compare notes in case we double up.' Returning to the table, she stirred milk and sugar into her coffee, then took a tentative sip. 'Mmm, that's good.' She smiled.

With a guilty pang, Jake remembered the envelope he'd thrown into his overnight bag. His daughter had given it to him just before he'd left. 'I've got a few things I thought she might like, but before I left she scribbled down some of her own recommendations in a letter addressed to both of us. We could look at it together later on, if you like?'

'Good idea…although she never asks for much.' Ailsa's amber eyes seemed faintly troubled for a moment. 'I know children are resilient… God knows they have to be sometimes, with the things they have to endure…bereavement, illness, divorce… But I worry that Saskia doesn't always tell me if something is bothering her. Do you ever get that impression?'

Because her observation echoed his own feelings about his daughter sometimes, Jake breathed out a long, considered breath before replying. 'I do. In fact, that was why I thought it was a good idea for her to spend some extra time with my mother. I think it's more likely that if she's troubled about anything she might find it easier confiding in her grandmother than telling us.'

'Sometimes it's so hard raising a child. I mean it's wonderful too, but when you're in bed at night you lie awake wondering if you've got it all wrong… You worry that you might have missed something vital that will significantly impinge on their lives later on. Do you know what I mean?'

It wasn't the easiest question in the world for him to answer, even though they had joint custody, because the lion's share of Saskia's care fell upon Ailsa. With every fibre of his being Jake wished it could be different. If only they had been able to ride out the terrible storm that came in the aftermath of the accident…if only they had— He cut the thought off short, impatient and angry with himself for even going there, because it was a soul-stealing exercise.

'I do… But at the end of the day it seems to me that all any parent can do is the best they can. If they love their child unconditionally, whatever happens, then it will work out.'

'I'm sure you're right.' Handing him his plate, Ailsa managed the briefest of uncertain smiles. 'Have your sandwich,' she urged. 'It's only ham and mustard—nothing terribly exciting. You must be famished.'

'You should eat yours too. You barely ate anything this morning.'

'Are you trying to fatten me up?' she joked.

He levelled a serious gaze at her. 'I wouldn't care what size you were as long as you were well and happy,' he said, low-voiced.

Responding with a sigh, Ailsa awkwardly dragged her glance away. 'I am well and I'm not unhappy… It's just that— Never mind.'

'What?'

'It's nothing…really.'

'Tell me.'

'I wish we had talked more when we were together, that's all. You were always so driven to make the family business even more successful that often it felt as if there wasn't room for much else in your life. Anyway… I don't want us to argue again, so I'll leave the subject alone for now. Let's just eat our food and drink our coffee, hmm?' Glancing out of the window, she gave an exaggerated shiver. 'All we have to do is just sit here in the warmth and look out at that winter wonderland, knowing we don't have to go anywhere or do anything very much.'

Uneasy at her disturbing admission of what she'd been musing on, Jake reluctantly agreed. 'Okay...if that's what you want.'

'You never were very good at relaxing.'

He lifted an eyebrow. 'Oh? And you *were*?'

'At least I could sit and knit—do something productive and relax at the same time.'

'I suppose you're going to suggest I take up knitting now?'

About to sip her coffee, Ailsa quickly put the mug down again, her hand against her chest as she fought to control the laughter that bubbled up inside her. *She failed.* 'That would have to be the funniest sight in the world,' she giggled.

'I'm glad you think so.' His lips twitching with the urge to give way to laughter himself, Jake just about managed to keep his expression on the stern side—but it wasn't easy.

As he stared back into the sparkling golden eyes across the table the sight of this pretty woman's enjoyment was more effective at demolishing his defences than anything else he could think of. It reminded him how often in the past a dark mood had been rescued by her humour. *It was another precious facet of her that he missed...* These days—except for when he was with his daughter—the dark moods were sadly more and more prevalent.

'Don't be so serious,' she scolded him cheerfully. 'Apparently men who take up knitting are on the increase.'

'Now you're going too far.' This time Jake couldn't hold back a grin. 'Besides...I don't have elegant, nimble fingers like you. My hands are too big to wield knitting needles!'

'Let me see.'

Before he could stop her, Ailsa reached for both his

palms and turned them over to examine them. The sharp intake of breath she exhaled made his heart turn over. She was staring at the vivid patchwork of scars that decorated his skin—some deep and jagged, others pale and thin.

'I'd forgotten about these,' she murmured softly.

He wanted to drag his hands back, keep them out of sight so as not to remind her of what had happened to them both, so as not to remind himself that he had failed in not keeping her and their baby safe. But Ailsa wouldn't let him drag them away. Instead she was lightly smoothing her fingers over the scars, and the touch of her infinitely soft skin was just too soothing and mesmerising for him to want to be free of it just then.

'I've always loved your hands, you know?' She looked straight into his eyes. 'It doesn't matter that they're scarred. They don't diminish you in any way, Jake. You got these scars because you were protecting me…they're heroic.'

His heart thumped hard. For a long moment a sensation of *white noise* prevented him from thinking straight. When he finally could, he snatched his hands away rubbing them almost with distaste. 'Heroic is the last thing they are,' he muttered angrily. 'Because at the end of the day I *didn't* protect you, did I?'

Ailsa's expression was stricken. 'It all happened so fast… It was like some horrific dream…a nightmare. What more could you have done? You did everything you could to protect me and the baby. You risked your life for us and got badly hurt in the process.'

Reaching for a sandwich, Jake took a bite—but it might as well have been cardboard, because his tastebuds were so deadened by anguish and regret that he couldn't even taste it.

Returning it to the plate, he shoved his chair away from the table and got up. At the door, he threw up his hands in a gesture of apology. 'I can't do this. I can't keep revisiting what happened. I only end up feeling like the whole of my life's been a waste of time.'

'That's dreadful. How could you even think such a terrible thing for even a moment? What about your daughter? How do you think *she'd* feel to hear you speak like that? As if you'd given up on everything? To maybe think she could never even have a chance of making you happy?'

Knowing that he'd hate for Saskia to hear him sounding so low, or to believe that her existence didn't mean the world to him, Jake forced himself to rally as he regarded the increasingly troubled look in Ailsa's eyes. 'Some hero, huh?' He grimaced. Then, turning away, he made his way back upstairs to his room...

CHAPTER SIX

Some hero, huh? Jake's self-deprecating comment hung in the air long after he'd left the room, making Ailsa feel like weeping.

He was a hero…he *was*! Fresh panic gripped her that she had been too hard on him at the time of the accident and during the long recuperation period they'd both endured afterwards. All her grief and anger at the loss of their baby and the realisation that she would never again bear children had been targeted at Jake. No wonder he'd wanted a divorce!

Her heart thumped hard. But then the difficult memory returned of how even before the accident their marriage had been in trouble. It had been just as she had described it to Jake earlier. They hadn't talked nearly enough because he was always working so hard. They'd never discussed what was most important to each other—never found out who they really were, what had shaped them into the people they were. They had simply left it to chance that somehow any difficulties would work themselves out and things would be good again.

The only place that Jake had truly revealed his feelings had been in bed. As wonderful as that had been, it hadn't been enough to help their relationship endure. They'd needed to build a foundation of honesty, respect and

truth that would carry them through the hard times. They
hadn't. One look into the desolate valley of his glance was
enough for Ailsa to realise that he had suffered greatly—
perhaps *beyond* endurance. She had no doubt that his father's death had added to that suffering.

She lightly thumped her breastbone to help release the
distress that threatened to gather force. If she did nothing else, she decided, Jake would walk away from here
knowing that she wasn't going to add to his suffering any
more—if Ailsa could just convince him that in future she
only wanted the best for him, that she forgave him for
the way things had worked out between them and genuinely regretted everything she'd ever said or done that had
wounded him, then maybe...maybe this time they could
at least part as friends?

Restless now, she wrapped the uneaten sandwiches and
stored them away in the refrigerator. Tonight she was determined to cook them a delicious meal that they would
both eat and enjoy. Maybe she could suggest it was a peace
offering—a new start for them both as friends? But even as
Ailsa turned the idea over in her head her stomach roiled
in protest. *She didn't just want to be Jake's friend... She
wanted... She wanted...*

With a heartfelt sigh she remembered the delicious
warmth of his seductive lips, how his hard body fitted
hers so perfectly—as if they'd been created just for each
other and nobody else. Then, like a blow she hadn't been
quick enough to duck, the memory of their baby growing inside her—of Jake pressing his lips to her belly each
night before they slept—cruelly returned and devastated
her all over again.

Choking back a sob, she found her anguished gaze captured by the fresh shower of delicately drifting snow outside the window. Hugging her arms over her chest, she let

her thoughts immediately turn to her living child...darling Saskia. Her racing heartbeat steadied. In a few more days she would be home again. And, however her daughter was spending the time with her grandmother, she hoped she was enjoying herself.

Adding a quick heartfelt prayer that she and Jake could somehow find a way of making the remaining time they had together before he left for Copenhagen less traumatic and much less wounding for them both, she reached for her favourite recipe book on the shelf above the fridge, already decided on the appetising dish she would make for dinner...

Opening his eyes to the darkened room, Jake realised he must have fallen asleep again. One minute he'd been lying on the bed, staring up at the beamed ceiling with his stomach churning and his thoughts racing, then the next...*bam!* He'd been out like a light. The emotional exhaustion that had regularly visited him since the accident had caught up with him again with a vengeance. It had laid him out with a punch worthy of a prize-fighter.

Sitting up, he scraped his fingers through his hair, then rubbed his chest because his heart ached. The dark and heavy sense of loss that sometimes imprisoned him when he awoke returned. *'Dear God...'* The harsh-voiced utterance sounded desolate even to his own ears. Accompanying his return to consciousness was another disturbing element. He might have been comatose but his heavy sleep hadn't been dreamless...not by a long chalk. His mind had been full of arresting images of Ailsa...of her incandescent amber gaze, her lustrous long hair, her 'pocket Venus' figure and flawless velvet skin. The most disturbing thing of all was that the images had been so erotically charged.

Right then Jake knew that if the roads weren't cleared

soon then he was going to be in trouble. Lusting after his beautiful ex-wife had not been one of the problems he'd envisaged when he'd decided to make this trip. *Why had she said those things to him, as if she still held some residue of feeling for him?* 'I've always loved your hands...' she'd admitted, then gently touched his scars as though she was far from repelled by them...as if they signified something almost precious...

Shaking his head with a groan, Jake swung his long jean clad legs over the side of the bed. The night was already drawing in, and he reached towards the lamp to turn it on and illuminate the gloom. If the temperature in the room hadn't been quite so chill he would have taken an ice-cold shower to help quell the searing ocean of need that his erotic dreams of Ailsa were making him drown in. As it was, now that he was fully awake he found himself concerned that she didn't have a better heating system in place.

For a few distracting seconds sexual need was overshadowed by irritation and frustration that she hadn't used some of the money he'd given her to live more comfortably. After all, there wasn't just herself to consider. Didn't their daughter deserve to benefit from her father's wealth too? he thought angrily.

She was cooking again. The most sumptuous aroma he could imagine was emanating from the kitchen as Jake walked down the stairs. His empty stomach growled hungrily. Ruefully he recalled that he hadn't eaten the sandwich Ailsa had made him earlier. She was stirring something in a generous-sized cast iron pot on the range cooker, her slim back to him as he entered the cosy, much warmer room.

But the first thing Jake asked didn't concern her cooking. 'Have you tried the phones again to see if there's any service?'

Laying down her wooden spoon on a nearby saucer, then smoothing her hands down over her ridiculously cheerful apron, Ailsa turned to him with a frown. 'I have. It's no-go, I'm afraid.'

'Pity.' The comment was uttered with more force than he'd intended.

'I'm sorry it's such disappointing news. Were you resting?' she asked lightly, clearly attempting to divert his sullen mood and proffering an unexpected smile. A near-*angelic* smile that made Jake feel like the very worst boor. 'You look a lot less tired than you did earlier.'

'What have you done to me? Drugged my coffee? Woven some kind of spell? I don't think I've slept so much in my entire life!'

Her smile didn't disappear. She gave a slight shrug of her slim shoulders, her serene expression the personification of kindness itself. 'Then it must be exactly what you needed. I'm envious. Don't knock it. I'm making us *coq au vin* for dinner tonight. I thought something more substantial as well as perhaps a bit more adventurous would be good.'

'I don't want you to spend all your time cooking for me. I'm not helpless. I can easily rustle something up for myself.'

'I'm sure you can.' Now her smile was a little tight-lipped, as if he had offended her. *He found himself cursing his boorish inability to be more amenable.* 'But I'm making a special meal as a kind of truce between us,' she continued, 'When the time comes for you to leave, I want you to know that you're welcome here if you should ever want to visit again.'

'Well, it doesn't look as if that time is coming any time soon…at least not tonight.'

Standing in front of the uncurtained window, Jake glanced up at the darkening skies and the lacy fall of snow that showed little sign of abating. It took him aback that Ailsa had asserted he was welcome if he ever wanted to return. Yet frustration gnawed at him that he wasn't yet able to head back to Copenhagen, as he'd planned, and sign off his work so that he could go and spend some time with Saskia and his mother. Even more frustration reigned because he wasn't able to corral the desire that automatically seized him whenever he was in the same vicinity as Ailsa. Just being in the same room was becoming a physical and emotional *torment* that tested him to the very edge of his reason.

'Dinner will be ready in about half an hour. The chicken is in the oven and I'm just making some vegetable soup for a starter. Would you mind going into the dining room and lighting some candles? If you need any spare you'll find them in the sideboard drawer.'

Did she know that he'd do anything she asked him right then—*even climb onto the roof and howl like a wolf*—just for the chance of a repeat showing of that sweet angelic smile she'd given him earlier?

Deliberately holding her gaze, Jake couldn't help grinning at the wild reaches of his imagination. 'Sure.'

'What's so funny? Have I got dirt on my nose or something?' Rubbing her face with the edge of her sleeve, she sounded vaguely upset.

'No. Your face is fine…perfect, in fact. I was just amused at what I'd be prepared to do to be on the receiving end of one of your smiles again.'

'Really?' Her voice dropped to an entranced whisper,

and the already slow and heavy primal beat in his blood throbbed even harder and headed devastatingly south.

'*Really...* Are the matches in the sideboard drawer too?'

'Yes, they are.'

'I'd better go and light the candles, then.'

Switching on the light as he entered the dining room, Jake moved towards the heavy mahogany sideboard where a pair of elegant silver candelabra stood. Blinking at them unseeingly for a moment, he took some deep slow breaths to reorientate himself. If he'd ever forgotten that Ailsa had the power to hold him in thrall with just a simple innocent glance, then he was forcefully reminded of that power now.

Distractedly, he opened a drawer to retrieve the box of matches that she'd told him he would find there. He'd just struck one when the dining room was suddenly plunged into darkness. An answering jolt leapt in the pit of his stomach. Touching the flame in turn to the candle-tips in front of him, he watched the fire's sensuous shadows weave and dance against the wall for hypnotic seconds before transporting the candelabra out into the hallway, almost bumping into an agitated Ailsa, who'd come to find him.

In the glow of the candle flames, her beautiful almond eyes were as bright and golden as a cat's. 'It must be a power cut. We haven't had one in ages, but we do get them out here from time to time.'

'Why doesn't that surprise me?' he answered. Because he hadn't been able to keep his growing desire for her in check, Jake failed to keep the irritation from his tone. 'Have you checked the fuse box?'

'It was the first thing I did. None of the switches have tripped, so it must be a power cut.'

'Take this.' Handing her one of the candelabrum, with its flickering trio of candles, he turned back into the dining room to collect its twin. Back in the dimmed hall-way, he said brusquely, 'Let's get back into the kitchen, shall we?'

'Thank goodness for the range cooker.' Returning to the stove, Ailsa resumed her stirring of the fragrant soup she was cooking. 'At least dinner won't be ruined.'

Setting his candelabrum down on the table, Jake moved to stand beside her. 'Is the stove oil-fired?'

'Yes.'

'So it supplies the central heating too?'

She stopped stirring the soup. Her smooth brow was distinctly worried as she turned to face him. 'I'm afraid not... But I've got the wood-burner in the living room. We can go and eat our dinner in there to keep warm, if you like?'

'When you've had these power cuts before, have they lasted long?'

'The last one lasted a whole day. It was a bit of a nui-sance because I lost all the food in the freezer. Apart from that...we managed.'

Jake bit back an accusing retort. He didn't have any say about where or *how* Ailsa chose to live any more—he knew that. But Saskia was a different matter. 'I can't say I'm en-amoured of the idea of you and our daughter just "man-aging". Don't you think that it's crazy, choosing to live in such an isolated place where you could potentially be cut off from the rest of the world for days in bad weather, and are prey to inconvenient losses of power that could leave you without heat and light for God knows how long?'

'That's a bit dramatic. They have power cuts in the city, as well you know. Besides...I've lived here for a long time now. I'm used to it and I like it.' Looking as though she wanted to embellish upon that statement, she chewed down on her lip instead and said nothing.

Jake sighed. 'You should at least see about getting your own generator, so you'll have back-up if this happens again. Look…this probably isn't the time to get you to think about moving somewhere less remote, but now that I've experienced what you and our daughter have to contend with for myself, I can't promise I'm going to leave the subject alone.'

Dropping down to a low cupboard next to the cooker, Ailsa retrieved two plain white dinner plates, along with a pair of matching soup bowls, and put them on the lowest oven shelf to warm them. As she straightened again, her previously pale cheeks were rosily flushed, Jake noticed. Was she angry at what he'd just said? If so, she'd clearly decided not to express it. *He wondered why.* The Ailsa he had known after the accident used to explode at the least little thing.

'We'll eat in here, shall we?' she suggested. 'The heat from the stove will keep us warm for a while.'

As she stole a furtive glance at the strong-boned, scarred, but still handsome visage on the other side of the table where they sat eating dinner, Ailsa was glad she hadn't irritably responded to Jake's declaration that she and Saskia should be living somewhere less remote. Having promised herself that she wouldn't add to his store of unhappiness, she meant to keep that vow. By the time he came to leave she wanted him to know that living 'out in the sticks', as it were, wasn't nearly as dreadful or inconvenient as he imagined. She also wanted him to realise that she was much more together than she'd used to be…that she was capable and strong and forging a good life for herself and their daughter after the unspeakable tragedy that had wounded and demoralised them all.

'I don't know what you saw in me when we first met.' The admission was out before she realised.

Laying down his fork, Jake steadily met her gaze across the candle flames. The midnight-blue lake that confronted her was so compelling that Ailsa's heartbeat all but thundered in her chest.

'That's easy. I saw a beautiful young woman who was shy and uncertain in an environment she clearly wasn't used to,' he answered, 'but who was so intent on doing a good job that it was endearing.' His rich voice was so low that she had to lean in to hear him.

'Shy and uncertain just about sums me up back then. I was so afraid of making a mistake that I practically jumped out of my skin every time the phone rang.'

'You left out beautiful.'

'What?'

'I said you were beautiful as well as shy and uncertain.'

She knotted her hands together. 'I never felt very beautiful…and I'm not looking for you to reassure me about that. The truth is I was stunned that someone like you would even glance at a girl like me.'

'Someone like me?'

'Yes—someone who seemed to have it all…looks, money, position. It really was hard for me to understand your interest in me.'

'You didn't see the eyes of the other men that followed you whenever you walked into a room?'

'No…I didn't.' *I only saw your eyes*, Ailsa admitted silently. From the very first time, when Jake had introduced himself to her, she'd been completely captivated by him. The other men that had walked through her days had been relegated to ghostlike figures of little substance in comparison.

'Why don't we take our drinks into the living room?

It's getting a little chilly in here and we can add another log to the burner,' he suggested, already on his feet.

Glancing distractedly down at her barely touched glass of wine, Ailsa felt her senses roar at the idea of spending the evening sitting by the fire with Jake, with nothing but the light of the dancing flames of fire and candle to illuminate the blackout.

Her hand shook a little as she curled it round the glass's crystal stem and stood up. 'Are you sure you only want to drink orange juice? You wouldn't prefer a glass of wine?' she asked, a husky catch in her voice.

A glimmer of a smile visited Jake's well-cut lips but was quickly gone again. 'I'm sure.'

'You don't enjoy it any more?'

'No.'

'Can I ask why?'

'I don't touch alcohol because I can't find pleasure in something potentially so destructive.'

The seductive warmth that had been curling deep into Ailsa's belly was suddenly replaced by ice-cold steel. She snatched her hand away from the wine glass as though a piece of it had sheared off and cut deep into her skin. 'You mean because that driver was drunk when he ploughed into us?'

A muscle flinched clearly in the cheek that was still smooth and unscarred. 'Yes. But I'm not saying that *you* shouldn't enjoy it. I'm sorry if I was too blunt.'

His meant-to-be consoling words didn't help. 'You weren't too blunt. I'd rather have the truth, no matter how hard it is to hear. I think there are too many sorrys between us…we've blamed each other for so much, Jake.'

He looked to be considering this comment for a long time. Then he breathed out a sigh and said, 'Let's go into

the living room, shall we? You take that candelabrum and
I'll bring the other one. Bring your wine too.'

'I don't want it now.'

'Bring it.' He lifted a gently chastising eyebrow.

Once they'd arranged the candles in the best positions
to light the room, Jake sat on one supremely comfortable
couch and Ailsa on the other. The mere fact that they'd
done that so automatically grieved her more than she could
say. Cradling the glass of wine she no longer had the slightest inclination to drink, she focused her sights on the fire
blazing in the burner rather than on her charismatic ex-
husband—even though her secret wish was to gaze at his
compelling features for the longest time. A disturbing
thought struck her. What if when they woke tomorrow
morning a thaw had taken place during the night, melting
the snow? *If so, there'd be no further need for him to stay...*

'Come back to me, Ailsa.'

'What?'

The smoky-voiced command jolted her. So much so
that she almost spilled her wine. In her heart, wild hope
tussled with a more pragmatic desire to be sensible.

'You went to a place where I couldn't reach you. I don't
like it when that happens. It worries me.'

'I—I was thinking what a shame it is that we can't
switch on the Christmas lights,' she lied. 'You worked so
hard fixing them up.'

'We'll switch them on tomorrow. It's not the end of the
world if we can't turn them on tonight.'

'No... It isn't. We've seen the end of the world, haven't
we?' Her voice faltered, dropped to a bare murmur.

The fresh applewood log Jake had added to the fire
crackled and hissed, and suddenly Ailsa was staring at
long straight legs in velvet-napped, expensive blue denim
as he came and planted his feet in front of her.

Gently, he took her glass and set it down on a nearby surface. 'Come here.'

She didn't argue. She didn't have the heart. Besides, how could she argue with the man she had built every dream of love and hope around? It felt like heaven having him so close, sensing his warm breath brush her face, having his long-lashed blue eyes command her attention like no one else's could.

As his glance roved across her fire-warmed features, it was perhaps the most intense that she'd ever seen it. The heat from his hands burned through the denim of her jeans as they settled round her hips. 'I wish you didn't hurt so much. It near kills me to think of you in pain in any way.'

'It's not your fault. It's just that sometimes—sometimes the most dreadful feelings wash over me…feelings stirred by the terrible memory of that car hitting us. I can still hear the ear-splitting sound of the car tyres skidding in the rain. Even when I tell myself that one day the memories and feelings will fade, because this hurt can't last for ever, I don't think I really believe it. Most of the time I try and stay positive…not let things get me down…especially for Saskia's sake. But then something reminds me, and the pain comes back and makes a liar of me.'

Jake's hands firmed round her hips and Ailsa swallowed hard.

'I just wish it was spring again, so that I could throw open all the windows and breathe more freely—do you know what I mean? Sometimes I feel so trapped it's as though I couldn't run far enough away to escape.' She sniffed, knowing that inside her emotions were helplessly unraveling. 'But of course I'm only trying to escape from myself.'

He didn't reply. He didn't have to. It was enough for her to know that he listened and understood. She exhaled a

breath that wasn't quite steady. Then he was kissing her—
kissing her as though the desire had erupted pure and un-
diluted straight from his soul. If there was the slightest
inclination in her to regain control then Ailsa willingly surrendered it. Beneath the onslaught of devastating emotion
and the wild, hungry need that her heart and body easily
matched she felt like the fragile frond of a willow, borne
on a hurricane into the drowning rapids of a thunderous
waterfall...

CHAPTER SEVEN

JAKE drew Ailsa down onto the couch behind them and never—not even for a moment—separated his mouth from her lips or his hands from her body. Hunger and desire long denied could no longer be contained. They cleaved to each other as though fearful another storm would batter them, separating them for ever this time...

Finding herself positioned beneath Jake's hard, heavier body, Ailsa greedily drove her fingers through the short silken strands of his hair, her senses bombarded by the twin scents of his arresting cologne and the deliciously musky male warmth that was his own personal blueprint. He raised his head to look at her. This time he didn't ask her if this was what she wanted. *There was no need.*

In the softly waving candlelight the strongly hewn features mesmerised her. Even his scar was beautiful, because it was an integral part of him now. And in spite of all that had happened he exuded such tenacity and strength. Ailsa sensed it. So how could even the cruellest wound mar or lessen such an indomitable presence?

She gently touched her palm to the side of his face. 'Jake...I want this as much as you do...I really do. But I haven't—I mean it's been a long time since I— What if I can't manage it any more?'

Her hand fell away and she curled it round his iron hard

bicep instead. The force of how much she wanted him took her breath away. Her blood was on fire just at the mere anticipation of him loving her as he'd used to. Yet the blunt truth was that she was scared...so *scared* that it would hurt or be too uncomfortable for her to endure. Her body had not healed overnight after being injured in the accident and losing the baby. It had taken weeks before she'd had the strength and confidence even to try to meet the normal demands of day-to-day life. If she now found herself physically unable to go through with this most intimate of acts between a man and a woman then she would disappoint and demoralise them both.

Her heart drummed hard as she waited for Jake's response. When she saw that his expression was the epitome of tenderness itself a huge weight lifted from her heart. The kindness reflected back at her softened the harsher contours of his face, turning his eyes to liquid silver in the dimmed light.

'We'll take it slowly,' he promised. 'The last thing in the world I want to do is hurt you. And if at any point you want to change your mind...well, that's okay too.'

Ailsa breathed a relieved sigh. Then she simply surrendered to the melting sensations that seemed to be intensifying deliciously inside her.

Item by item Jake carefully undressed her. In between removing her clothing he tenderly kissed every inch of flesh that was revealed. She shivered and shook with the sheer joy and pleasure of it. When he removed his own sweater and the tee shirt underneath, her gaze appreciatively luxuriated in the jaw-dropping male physique whose mouth-watering appeal had not dimmed at all in the passing years. Yes, there were a few nicks and scars that hadn't been there before the accident, but—like the healed gash on his face—they didn't detract one iota from his power-ful attraction.

His shoulders and torso were lean and muscular—like an athlete's—and he had a very light dusting of dark blond hair crossing his chest. As she had glimpsed before, when his tee shirt had ridden up, Ailsa saw that even though Jake was a businessman—by dint of his career working in of-fices most days—he kept himself in good shape.

All thought was dizzyingly suspended when he touched his lips to her breast and drew the aching, rigid tip deep into the molten cavern of his mouth. Her womb gave an answering leap. He slid his hand down over her ribcage, the provocative trail his fingers took leading straight to the apex of her slender thighs. Gently but firmly he nudged them apart. When he started to explore the moist heat at her core she immediately tensed and grabbed his hand.

'Is it too much too soon? Am I hurting you?' Jake husked, lifting his head to examine her face concernedly.

Unable to relax and completely enjoy an experience she'd privately longed for and fantasised about through-out the years—even though fireworks were exploding in-side her at his touch—Ailsa pursed her lips. She shook her head. 'No. I'm just a bit tense in case—in case it does hurt,' she confessed anxiously.

He emitted a grated breath. 'Did the doctor tell you that it might?'

'She told me I might be sore…but that was about three months after the accident. And by that time we'd stopped being intimate, so I never—I never found out whether it hurt or not.'

'It's been over four years since then.'

The silvery-blue eyes boring down at her were like haunting starlight, and Ailsa's stomach turned over at the sorrow she saw glinting in their depths. That ravaged glance made up her mind.

'I know,' she whispered. Carefully cupping her hand behind his neck, she pulled his face back down to hers. 'Try again,' she urged softly, tracing the outline of his lips with her fingertip. 'Everything will be okay.'

He hesitated. 'Are you sure?'

'Yes.'

As if to confirm her decision, her hips automatically softened and her body relaxed. This time when Jake explored her she sensed urgency and a need for fulfilment take hold of her almost straight away. There was no pain, as she'd feared there might be. Instead there was a sensual and erotic blaze of heat that built and built, until her teeth clamped down on her lip because it was almost too incredible to bear, and as the sensations reached a crescendo a throaty moan of pleasure she couldn't hold back escaped her.

Before she recovered Jake kissed her again, his silken tongue gliding into her mouth with a similar urgent need to experience the bliss and fulfilment that Ailsa had just enjoyed. Dizzingly giving herself up to his wonderful kiss without reservation, she sensed him press himself inside her and then thrust deeply upwards. Again there was no pain—just an amazingly pleasurable fullness she knew straight away she'd missed and achingly mourned. She wrapped her slender legs round his lean, hard middle to welcome him in even deeper. As he thrust into her again and again her hands clung onto the broad banks of his shoulders and her fingernails bit into the smooth muscle of his back. For a second time she came undone. Only a few moments later Jake anchored her head with his hands and with a harsh-voiced groan helplessly joined her...

As soon as he came back down to earth and the reality

of what he'd just done hit it wasn't the fact that he'd spilled his seed unprotected inside Ailsa that was Jake's concern. Because sorrowfully, to his cost, he knew that she couldn't become pregnant. He was concerned that he'd maybe been too forceful and hurt her. But then he saw that her sweet, entrancing lips were curved into a wistful contented smile, and it raised his hopes to the skies.

With growing wonder he cupped the side of her face beneath the silken waterfall of her lovely hair to tenderly stroke the pad of his thumb across her cheek. 'You look happy,' he said.

'That's because I feel good…*very* good.'

'I didn't hurt you, then?'

'No, you didn't. My body feels like it's healed completely. It's just such a wonderful revelation that I can function normally again. I suppose the worry that I couldn't has been playing on my mind for a long time now.'

'Maybe you should have gone to a doctor to have her properly check you over and reassure you?'

'You know how I feel about doctors.'

'Even so, having an examination could have saved you a lot of heartache.'

'Point taken.'

'I'll drop the subject, then.'

On the wall behind them, the sinuous shadow of the candle flames continued to dance and weave, and the fire in the wood burning stove seemed to blaze more brightly than before. With a silent prayer, Jake thanked the powers that be for the unexpected gift of a blackout. Then he carefully withdrew from the incomparable delights of Ailsa's body and reached for the substantial plaid woollen throw on the back of the couch to pull it over them both.

'Cosy, huh?' he said, grinning as he urged her close into his side.

'It feels seriously decadent,' she agreed, screwing up her nose.

Her amber-coloured eyes were delightfully mischievous. *It had been a long time since Jake had seen her looking so untroubled...like the Ailsa of old that he had fallen head over heels in love with a lifetime ago...*

'So when was the last time you felt as decadent as this, hmm?'

'I think it was when you whisked me away from work in the lunch hour one day and took me to the Hilton where you'd rented a room for just the afternoon.' Her lashes lowered shyly for a moment. 'We made love for the longest time. Normally I would have feared being sacked, returning to work so late, but seeing as I was with the boss's son...'

'Didn't I promote you after that?' he teased.

She playfully slapped him on the arm. 'No, you didn't! And if you'd tried I would have vehemently protested.'

'No, you wouldn't.'

'Yes, I would.'

'I agree. You probably would have. You were always far too conscientious for your own good.' He dropped a lingering warm kiss onto her mouth and she went very still. 'We had fun together once upon a time, didn't we?' he mused softly.

'You were very passionate.'

'I still am.' He noticed wariness creep into her eyes at that comment, but in the next instant it was gone again.

'Jake?'

'Yes?'

'Why did you wait so long to meet up with me again? I mean...four years of telephone calls making arrangements for Saskia to stay with you every other weekend, then sending Alain to pick her up and bring her home instead of doing it yourself. I know you have to work, but would it have been so inconvenient for you to collect her and bring her home to me?'

'It's not that it was inconvenient. It was that— Look, do we have to talk about this right now?'

Fiercely resisting breaking the spell of these precious intimate moments, Jake feared another soul-destroying disagreement if they fell into discussing how they'd conducted things in the past. He really didn't want to reveal the guilt and shattering disappointment that dogged him still for not protecting her and the baby that terrible night. Neither did he want to confess that he saw it as his punishment to stay away from her. That was why he employed Alain to act as go-between—not because it was too inconvenient for him to get away from work.

He and Ailsa had just made love, and it had been beyond wonderful, but he knew it didn't make everything all right. *How could it when his mind, body and spirit were weighed down with enough crippling guilt to sink a battleship?*

With a sleepy smile, Ailsa dreamily stroked his arm. 'No. We don't have to talk about it now if you don't want to. But I'd really like us to talk tomorrow and maybe clear a few things up.'

'Okay.' Jake fought the reluctance that her suggestion inevitably caused, containing his feelings to try and protect himself and silently conceding that maybe it *was* time to tell her a bit more about himself and why he struggled so hard with expressing his emotions. He brought her fingertips up to his lips and kissed them. 'Why don't you close your eyes for a while, hmm? You look a little tired.'

Letting her head rest against his chest, she concurred. 'I *am* tired—though goodness knows why, when I've done very little today. Don't let the fire go out, will you?'

she murmured, already drifting off into a land where he couldn't follow.

'I won't.' Swallowing down the ache inside his throat, he settled his arm around her shoulders. Then, staring over at the wood stove, he surrendered to the hypnotism of the still dancing flames...

'What was that?' Staring wildly round in the semi-dark a few hours later, Ailsa pushed herself up. The haunting sound that had pierced her sleep still echoed disturbingly in her mind. 'It sounded like a baby crying.'

'It wasn't a baby.' Crouched low in front of the burner, where he'd obviously been stoking the fire, his torso bare, Jake got to his feet. 'I think it was a fox,' he said, turning to face her.

His jeans were riding low across his hips, highlighting the ridged toned muscle of his flat stomach, and his voice was 'just woken from sleep' husky. She couldn't imagine any other man looking more dangerously sexy. In a disturbing flash she remembered why they were still there in the darkened front room, sensed the places on her body where he'd intimately touched her. That instigated a deep and powerful ache for more of his passionate attentions.

Then, realising she was as bare as a newborn babe beneath the throw, she tugged the cover self-consciously up around her shoulders.

'A fox?' She rubbed her eyes and blinked at him.

'We're deep in the heart of the countryside. It's not unusual. We even have them in London.'

'That's why I don't keep chickens.'

'Really? You mean you *wanted* to keep chickens?'

Ailsa saw that Jake was shamelessly grinning, perhaps mocking the notion that she had such ordinary, mundane ambitions these days. *It certainly didn't sit easily with the luxurious lifestyle she'd once enjoyed as his wife.*

'I did. What's wrong with that?'

His expression sobering, Jake lifted his shoulders and dropped them again. 'I didn't say there was anything wrong with it. You're quite the little country girl these days, aren't you?'

She felt her face heat at the observation. 'It's quieter here than the city, and consequently I feel less stressed.'

'Well…talking of lessening your stress, I think you should try and get a bit more sleep. It's only just after three a.m.'

'The power hasn't come back on yet?'

'I haven't checked. I've just been enjoying the candle-light and the glow from the fire.'

His concentrated sleepy-eyed glance instigated an outbreak of goosebumps all over her body. 'I prefer that too,' she murmured, snuggling back down under the throw.

Immediately crossing the carpet to the light switch, Jake flicked it on. The electric light failed to register. Shaking his head, he made his way back to the fire. 'If the phones are back on in the morning I'll make some calls and see about organising that generator.'

'You don't have to do that.'

'I know I don't *have* to. I *want* to… There's a difference.'

'Yes…' Ailsa agreed sleepily, nervously wondering if he was going to rejoin her in their makeshift bed on the couch any time soon. She realised she'd be very happy if he did… 'There is a difference.'

As if intuiting her secret wish, he dropped down beside her, at the same time raking his fingers through hair that had clearly received similar rough treatment earlier.

'I like this "just got out of bed" look,' she teased him.

Unable to understand why it should happen right then, Jake stared into Ailsa's smiling beautiful face and felt a powerful resurgence of grief at what he had lost. Sometimes he seriously wondered if sorrow was the price he had to pay for this life even for the briefest moment of pleasure. If so, the trade-off was a cruel one. *For him, the death of their baby and the death of his marriage had signalled the end of love...period.*

Coiling a gleaming strand of her chestnut hair round his finger, dredging up a smile from God only knew where, he stayed where he was for only a minute more, suddenly knowing that he wouldn't be spending the rest of the night there on the couch with her. He wouldn't renege on his silent promise to reveal to her why he found it so hard to express his true emotions, but right now he knew he needed some space to think things through.

'Rock stars would give their eye teeth for inside information on how I do it so effortlessly,' he replied drolly.

'Are you okay? Why were you up? Did the sound of the fox wake you too?'

'No. I just naturally woke up, then saw that the fire was dying.'

'You look tired, Jake. Why don't you come and join me under the covers...lie down for a while?'

Feeling as though he had lead in his heart, he shook his head. In another second he was up on his feet again. 'I think I need to get back to my bed upstairs...we'll both sleep better if I do. I've stoked the fire, so it should keep you warm for a while yet. Like I said, in the morning, if the phone lines are working, I'll sort out getting you a generator. Goodnight, Ailsa...try and get some more sleep, hmm?'

Collecting the remainder of his clothes from where they lay strewn on the carpet, he exited the room without so much as a backward glance. But the disturbing memory of Ailsa's surprised and saddened face weighed heavily on his tread as he climbed the staircase in the dark to return to his room...

A dazzling ray of sunlight arrowed through the window, and outside, where a blanket of snow covered everything in sight, it had the dramatic effect of making the crystalline white carpet shimmer like diamonds. And even as she stood there in the kitchen, gazing out at the magical wintry scene, Ailsa heard the sound of ice dripping from the eaves. *It was beginning to melt.*

She ought to be overjoyed, but she wasn't. The possibility of the chill weather changing for the better left her feeling raw and empty inside. *When he left, would it be another four years before she saw Jake again?* She'd found a note from him on the kitchen table. It read that the electricity had returned, and so had the service on the house phone. He'd gone out for a walk, but would be back soon to sort out the business of a generator and to make some calls home to Copenhagen.

He must have got up especially early, Ailsa realized, because by the time she'd arrived in the kitchen to sort out the detritus from last night's dinner the dishwasher had been almost at the end of its cycle. She had to confess it was a pleasurable surprise to find everything cleared and tidied away.

Moving across to the table, to lay out the crockery for breakfast, she grimaced and rubbed her back. Her muscles were seriously stiff from her night spent on the living room couch. *Pocket sprung mattress it was not!* But the main discomfort she was suffering was in the region of her heart, because Jake had left her there alone. *Why hadn't he stayed with her?* Was he afraid that now that they had been intimate she would make some sort of unreasonable demand on him?

To bring a temporary end to the string of apprehensive thoughts that were gathering with disturbing momentum as she stood there, she made a beeline for the telephone. Less than a minute later the warmly reassuring voice of Tilda Larsen sounded in her ear. Taken aback by the pleasure Jake's mother expressed at hearing from her, Ailsa once more conveyed her condolences on the death of her husband and asked how she was coping. Hearing that she was just taking one day at a time—because what else could she do?—Ailsa felt her heart go out to her. Then, unable to wait a moment longer, she asked to speak to her daughter.

'She's right here beside me,' Tilda replied affectionately. 'The little angel has been longing to talk to you.'

'Hello, Mummy—I've really missed you!'

'Hello, my darling. I've missed you too…so much. But the snow has been so heavy here that we couldn't get the phone to work and ring you. Are you all right?'

'I'm fine. I've been having a lovely time with Grandma. You don't mind me—staying a bit longer, do you?'

Ailsa's throat swelled. 'Of course I don't mind. I'm sure it's been a great help to her to have you there'

'Is Papa still with you?' Saskia asked.

Picking up on the longing in the childish tones, Ailsa sensed her stomach clench tight. 'Yes, he's still here, sweetheart. He's had to stay with me because the snow is so bad that he can't make it back to the airport. That's why he hasn't been able to return to Copenhagen yet.'

'You haven't been fighting?'

The question was like a thunderbolt, arrowing down out of the sky, exploding shards of electricity at her feet. 'Why do you ask that?'

At the other end of the line there was a brief pause, followed by a lengthy sigh. 'It's just that whenever you talk about Papa you get sad, and whenever he talks about you he sounds angry. I hope you don't get in a fight. It's nearly Christmas and I want you both to be happy.'

'Darling, I—we're neither of us unhappy, I promise you. And nor will we get in a fight.' Biting back the near-overwhelming urge to cry, Ailsa started in surprise when at the very moment Jake came in through the back door.

Having already divested himself of his outdoor clothing, he clapped his hands together to warm them and threw her a disarming grin. His cheeks were ruddy from the biting winter wind and his eyes mirrored the electric blue of a cloudless summer sky. A second lightning strike exploded through her insides.

'Mummy, are you still there?'

'Of course I am, darling. Papa is back from his walk. Do you want to say hello?'

'Yes, please!'

'It's Saskia,' she said quietly, her hand over the phone's mouthpiece.

Jake was at her side in an instant, and all but snatched the receiver from her. 'Is that you, baby?' she heard him ask huskily, and knew she didn't imagine the slight break caused by emotion in his meltingly rich voice.

CHAPTER EIGHT

UNABLE to keep the hurt and anxiety from her tone after they'd both completed their conversations with Saskia, Ailsa tackled Jake about the worrying comment their daughter had made expressing her concern that they might 'get in a fight'.

'Why would she say something like that?' she demanded, hugging her arms round the hip length, black angora sweater she'd matched with leggings. 'She said that you sound angry when you talk about me.'

'She's never mentioned that to me before.' His expression was immediately guarded, she noticed, almost drawn, as if this was an added complication he didn't want to discuss. 'If I've ever sounded angry it was probably because I was tired or stressing over something at work. I've certainly never been aware that I've conveyed anger towards you in her presence.'

'Well, Saskia is a very intuitive child. I'm sure she wouldn't have imagined it.' Her fingers were trembling a little as they brushed her hair back from her face, and beneath her ribs Ailsa's heart was galloping. 'She also said that I sound sad whenever I talk about *you*.'

His lips twisted ironically. 'Now, *there's* a surprise.'

'What do you mean?'

'I'm sure the thought of me doesn't exactly fill you with

joy. You must have plenty of regrets about how things worked out. In truth, apart from giving you Saskia, I must be the biggest mistake you ever made! All you ever wanted was a family, you told me once…but I even managed to screw that up for you.'

His tone was savage, his expression bleak. Shock eddied through her as though she'd stumbled into a ravine. She was dizzy with fear that the situation would only deteriorate if she didn't find a way of rescuing it somehow. The need to talk things out had never been more urgent.

She swallowed hard. 'I've never seen being with you as a mistake…*ever*. How could you believe such a crazy thing? And you didn't screw anything up either. Was it *your* fault that that man was over the limit that night? Of course it wasn't! Look, Jake…whatever personal hurts or damaging beliefs we're carrying around about each other, don't you think it's time we aired them so that we can let them go and move on? It was a dreadful thing to lose our baby, but does that mean we should stop fully living? Stay static in some kind of frozen animation for the rest of our lives and never enjoy happiness again? I don't think so. Besides…we have a daughter to think about as well as ourselves. I don't know about you, but I've had enough of grief and sadness. I want to find a better way. I certainly don't want our daughter growing up thinking that all we've done since the accident is blame each other for everything going wrong. That would be a horrible legacy.'

'I don't blame you for anything.'

'No? Then why would you be angry with me? Why did you go back to your own bed in the middle of the night? That looks very much like you weren't happy about something. Was it something I said? First you make love to me—then you shun me.'

'I didn't shun you.'

Jake looked distinctly uncomfortable. As if he might walk out at any second. In her mind, Ailsa implored him to stay. In the next instant the tension that emanated from his whole being seemed to dissipate—just as if he'd overcome his resistance for a deeper conversation and was now resigned to at least *some* discussion on the matter.

'It wasn't about anything you've done or said, Ailsa...I want you to know that. If I blame anyone for the situation between us it's myself, and if it's distressing Saskia because she's picking up vibes that I'm holding on to some kind of anger about the past then clearly we have to do something about it... *I* have to do something about it... I agree.'

The silence that followed Jake's surprising remark prickled with assorted tensions. He might have agreed they had to reconcile the past in some way, but Ailsa easily sensed the wealth of pain behind his words and the feeling that he was struggling to get a grip on it. She realised she would have to steer the ship.

'Jake? We'd run into problems in our marriage long before the accident. Let's be honest about that. That's probably why you're still angry. We never got to the bottom of our unhappiness then and we're still avoiding the issue now. The accident just brought things to a horrible head.'

'You're right.' His glittering gaze held her in a trance for several electrifying seconds before she reminded herself to breathe again. 'You know what I think part of the problem was?'

Ailsa stared. 'Tell me.'

'I put work before my family. I worked hard not for more money, position or acclaim, but because I craved my father's love and approval above all else. I never felt like I'd ever really had it...even as a child. He was a tough man to get close to. The hoops I'd put myself through to even win a smile from him you wouldn't believe! I'm afraid I got so blinded by the need to win his regard that I thought that if I worked harder, became more important to the success of the business than anyone else, then that would help me reach my goal. When you used to try and get me to talk about things, to tell you how I was feeling...I resisted at every opportunity. Even though I sensed the tension between us getting worse, I somehow convinced myself that things weren't really as bad as I imagined... I told myself that I could carry on behaving like some...some driven automaton and everything would still turn out all right. My father was a workaholic and I adopted the same soul-destroying pattern.

'Why couldn't I see it? Why couldn't I see that my obsession was hurting my family? Hurting *us*, Ailsa? I loved you so much. Except I didn't really demonstrate that to you, did I? Even when you found out you were pregnant with our son I still didn't take the time to get closer to you...except in bed, of course. I'm so sorry. I behaved like the classic emotionless macho male and I want you to know that I'm not proud of it.'

Ailsa was so overcome by what he'd said that she didn't know how to respond. Her body had no such dilemma. Unbidden, a purely primal desire for him to take her to bed drowned out any other thought or feeling. In all the years she had known him Jake had never spoken to her so frankly and honestly about his feelings. Suddenly the behaviour he'd exhibited during the dying days of their marriage—even before the accident—made so much sense. Having been raised without the love or approval or a parent herself, it wasn't hard for her to understand why Jake had been so constantly driven to win his father's regard. He was right. Jacob Larsen had been a good man, but he had definitely kept up a shield in front of his emotions.

How she wished that Jake had really been able to understand the depth of her love…had realised how it might have helped him. It probably wouldn't have healed his sense of hurt around his father, but it might have gone some way to helping him make peace with it and letting him concentrate on the people in his life he meant the world to instead. A wave of heat suffused Ailsa at the spine-tingling memory of the candlelit passion they'd shared last night. But, as compelling as the idea of making love was, she didn't want to bring their frank conversation to an end just yet.

'I'm sorry too, Jake. If you'd shared some of this with me back then we might have been able to deal with things better. In any case, I'm not exactly the innocent party. You suggested that perhaps I was too young to get married early on. Maybe you were right…not because I didn't genuinely love you or want to be with you, but because I too was looking for the love and the sense of belonging that I didn't have in my childhood and I projected all that need onto you. It was probably a heavy burden.

'It wasn't your job to make me happy or to give me a sense of worth, but when you worked late night after night, weekend after weekend, I told myself it was because I wasn't enough of a woman for you…that I must be lacking in some of the qualities a man needed in a wife because if I had them then you would be home more. The trouble was I had no real sense of myself as a worthwhile person at all, and you working all the time didn't help lessen that. I thought marriage was the answer for me because I was afraid to be alone. Yet I'd spent most of my life until I met you on my own! I've realised I'm perhaps more resilient than I believed. Starting the craft business and taking care of Saskia has shown me that.' Her lips formed a shy smile. 'I don't regret the time I spent with you Jake…even the sad and difficult days. I don't regret it one bit. I want you to know that.'

The statement didn't seem to reassure him. His steady gaze was definitely troubled. 'So where does all this leave us?' he asked.

'Well…at least we're being real with each other at last, don't you think? By the time you leave here at least you'll know that we've been honest with each other…that we're both dedicated to making the future different…to making it *better*.'

With another shaky smile she turned away, her aim to fill the kettle and make tea for her and coffee for Jake— anything to take her mind off the provocative track of getting close to him where it seemed disturbingly to want to linger.

What Ailsa wasn't prepared for was for Jake to step up behind her and draw her body firmly back against his. *Had he somehow read her mind?* The sensation of steely male warmth behind her made her insides melt. Lifting her hair off the back of her neck, he pressed his lips against the place he'd exposed, and although they were chilled from his winter stroll, the heat they injected into her bloodstream was near volcanic.

'What are you—?' The rest of her question helplessly died away as he laid his hand over her breast and cupped it.

'It might not fix anything or put everything right… but I can't help how I feel and right now I want you,' he breathed, the volatile words emitted on a throaty rasp as he slid his other hand inside the waistband of her leggings and then down—right down inside her cotton panties. 'I want you so bad I can hardly think about anything else…'

The answering gasp Ailsa emitted turned into a ragged whimper. Her whole body trembling with mindless need, she turned in his arms and the ravenous collision of mouths, teeth and tongues that followed turned the bones in her legs to running rapids that seriously threatened to unbalance her.

'I think what we need is a nice soft bed...don't you?'

She'd barely uttered, 'Mmm...' before Jake scooped her up in his arms as though she weighed not much more than one of the bundles of fabric she kept in her workroom and headed out into the hallway. She hung on with her arms round his neck, dropping incendiary little kisses onto his face and mouth as they travelled, even onto his indomitable chin with its sexy little cleft.

His intent burning gaze held hers all the way up the stairs to the guest bedroom. By the time he laid her down on the bed, with the ochre and scarlet silk eiderdown that she had crafted over a period of several months during a dry spell in her work, Ailsa was so consumed by longing and desire that her awareness of anything else but Jake simply dissolved...became utterly unimportant.

Staring up at him as he straddled her, she felt her focus intensify. Such deliberate examination at close quarters reacquainted her intimately with the features she had fallen in love with all those years ago. It didn't matter that time and tragedy had left their mark on them. Nothing could detract from the beauty of the precisely carved face and the blue eyes that were a sunlit lake one minute and a sultry moonlit night the next. Then there was the strongly defined nose that on a less handsome man might not be seen as an attribute but on Jake was simply absolutely right. But it was his mouth that she fixated on, because with a frisson of delicious anticipation she intimately knew the kind of immeasurable delights it could bestow...

In the otherwise silent room, Ailsa was suddenly very much aware of her own heightened breathing. *They didn't talk...* Words could come later, but for now their bodies would do the talking instead.

As her lover sat astride her, he jettisoned his sweater and tee shirt, then leant forward to tug her angora jumper over her head. As soon as he'd got rid of it he lowered his dark blond head to draw an aching rigid nipple into his mouth through the filmy gauze and cotton of her bra. The pleasure was so intense, the force of it far beyond mere words, that tears welled in her eyes. She couldn't begin to express how much she'd missed him. Over the years since they'd separated, when the thought of him caught her un-awares—for instance when she was out shopping or work-ing at her crafts or cleaning the house—it would instigate a deep ache of longing in the pit of her stomach that made her want to weep a veritable ocean of tears. Now, every-thing inside her burned for his possession.

Freeing her tingling breasts completely from her bra, Jake turned his attention to the rest of her clothing, and Ailsa luxuriated in the feeling of his hands moving impa-tiently over her skin. When she was naked beneath him, she eagerly wove her slender arms round his strongly corded neck as their lips hungrily met for another scald-ing kiss.

His senses were consumed with an awareness of every-thing about her that he'd loved and missed...the unique se-ductive scent of her body that was an aphrodisiac above all others, the beautiful long hair that resembled spun silk as it splayed out in chestnut waves on the pillow behind her, the almond-shaped amber eyes that needed no make-up in order for them to be sexy or appealing because they already had those attributes in abundance. Even the sight of the tiny mole behind her earlobe aroused his passion.

Jake had never fantasised about an ideal type when it came to women. He'd never preferred blondes over

brunettes or vice versa, or tall and slim over shorter and
more diminutive. Ticking boxes had never come into it. But
if the idea of the perfect woman *had* ever unconsciously
entered his daydreams, then surely Ailsa was it?

The fire in his loins reaching a near inferno of longing,
he started to ease himself inside her. Unable to hold back
the need to be closer, he pressed deep, then deeper still. It
was as if his entire body became the living beating heart
that throbbed so passionately in his chest. Ailsa's softly
arousing moans filled the air and Jake filled his hands with
her small pert breasts, before drawing them into his mouth
and then running his tongue over the firm satin buds at
their tip. Outside it might be the dead of winter, but here
in this soft warm bed it was a sultry Indian summer.

The lithe shapely body beneath him stilled suddenly.
The incandescent amber gaze darkened. The hot silken
purse that enveloped him clenched him tight again and
again. 'Jake…' She whispered his name as though caught
up in a spell, then drew him down to her again, buried her
face in the hollow between his neck and shoulder.

The stunning thought that he must have done something
good he wasn't aware of to be rewarded with the pleasure
of loving this incredible woman again crept up on him.
The fresh realisation that she was the mother of his precious child hit him squarely in his gut, awakening almost
primal feelings of possession and pride. This was Ailsa…
the woman who'd stirred a wealth of passionate emotion
in him he'd hardly known he possessed almost on sight…
the woman who might have borne him a son if only—

He wasn't quick enough to cut off the tide of pain and
fury that accompanied the agonising memory. The power
of it caught him on the raw and he thrust inside her so deep
that his volatile feelings spilled over into his passion, his
body jolting helplessly, as though swept away by a furious

current. In that drowning moment he surrendered all desire for control, simply let the force that carried him take
him straight to the dizzying heart of its power. The feral
cry that poured straight from his lungs when he got there
was like a savage shout of pain. What shocked Jake even
more was that as he cried out boiling tears submerged his
eyes.

Breathing hard, he lowered his head, desperately trying
to recover some composure, turning his face away from
Ailsa so she wouldn't see the evidence of his distress. But
the consoling gentle hand on his forearm and the deep sigh
that made the tiny hairs covering his skin immediately
stand to attention told him that she *did* see.

'What's wrong? Jake, tell me *please*.'

He didn't answer straight away. Still breathing hard, he
lifted his body from hers. Moving to the side of the bed, he
leaned over to reach for his discarded jeans. Delving into
a back pocket, he removed his calf leather wallet. Hesitating for only a moment, he extricated the grainy black and
white print he kept in one of the sections and handed it to
her.

'I just got to thinking about our son…*Thomas.* It was
an early summer's afternoon in Copenhagen when we—
when we made him…remember? Not long after that we
discovered you were pregnant. I kept the ultrasound photo
you gave me after we'd been to the clinic. You see? I didn't
forget him. How could I? He was—he was my boy…the
boy I didn't get to see grow up…'

'Oh, Jake…Jake…'

'Remember how ecstatic we were when we found out
the sex of the baby? We couldn't believe how lucky we
were to have a boy and a girl…the perfect little family.'

'I know you didn't forget him.' Her hair falling round
her face as she moved up onto her knees, Ailsa sounded

seriously shaken and Jake saw that her eyes were bathed in tears. 'I never knew you kept this. I'm sorry if I ever gave you the impression that I thought you didn't care about our baby as much as I do.'

'Maybe it was my fault because I never talked about it? It's the way I was taught. Not by my mother, but by my father. He had the belief that it showed strength of character if a man kept his feelings to himself. My mother was the only one he ever let his guard down with, and even then probably not very often. Anyway, he's gone too now and it's all water under the bridge. He's not coming back and neither is our son. And I can't keep going back there…to that cold, dark time when we lost Thomas. It's too hard. Can I have that?' Swallowing across the pain inside his throat, Jake leaned forward to take the picture. Then he carefully returned it to his wallet. Shoving it back down into his jeans pocket, he lifted his head, his gaze squarely meeting Ailsa's. 'The other thing I can't forget is how hurt you were. The sound of you crying out still haunts me.'

'You were hurt too.'

Almost afraid to see the compassion in her eyes, he was all but ready to dismiss it. *How could he possibly be deserving of care or compassion after what he'd done?* he wondered. During the last six months, since he had become CEO of the company, due to his hard work and dedication their profits had gone through the roof—but he didn't feel as proud of the fact as he once might have done. He'd just made one sacrifice too many to take any pleasure in it. And the burden of guilt at not protecting Ailsa and the baby seemed to grow heavier year by year, instead of lessening. Somehow he had to start to ease that burden. He didn't exactly know *how*, but at least he was open to entertaining the idea at last.

'It was a tough time for both of us,' he remarked quietly. 'But, like you said earlier when we spoke about the legacy we might be leaving Saskia, we have to find a way of moving on...agreed?'

'Agreed.'

Ailsa's smile was tinged with sadness, but hope also lingered in the softened amber glance Jake saw. Climbing back onto the bed, he gently took her into his arms. 'We'll stay here for a while, hmm?' he suggested, dropping a warm kiss on the top of her head. 'And when we're ready we'll talk some more.'

The promised continued conversation didn't ever manifest itself. Just a few minutes after Jake had folded Ailsa against his chest the sound of someone hammering on the front door made them guiltily spring apart.

'Who can that be?'

'I'm sorry, baby, but I'm not psychic. Why don't you go and see? And when you find out, tell them you're busy.'

Ailsa's heart pounded—not just with shock at the unexpected sound of the door knocker shattering the peace that had enveloped them, but because of the possessive inflection she clearly heard in Jake's tone.

'Were the roads any clearer when you went out this morning?' she asked him urgently, even as she reached for her discarded clothes and hastily pulled them on—not the easiest thing to accomplish when his blue eyes were observing her bare form with a hotly lascivious glint. 'I mean...were there any signs that there might be vehicles getting through?'

'The ice was melting a little, but I didn't see any car tracks. If it does thaw tonight then I can probably get to the airport tomorrow and catch a flight home. Who do you think is at the door? Not that ever so helpful neighbour of yours again, I hope?'

Silently reeling at the idea of Jake leaving the next day,

Ailsa took a second to get her bearings. 'If it is Linus then I don't want you to be rude to him. Why don't you just wait here? I'll be—I'll be back in a minute.'

As she self-consciously tucked her hair behind her ear, due to the disconcerting interest Jake was still displaying in her body, Ailsa prayed that it wasn't Linus calling. If it *was* she hoped she could quickly get rid of him—particularly if Jake decided to come downstairs…

His thick dark hair looking as though a comb had subdued the naturally curling locks especially for his visit, Linus surveyed Ailsa warmly as she opened the door. She had no control over the guilty blush that heated her cheeks. How could she when she'd just got out of bed with Jake?

'Linus…is everything all right?'

'I was going to ask you the same question,' he came back, jerking his head briefly behind him. 'I see the Range Rover's still here. Your ex hasn't gone back to Copenhagen yet, then?'

She frowned, then folded her arms across her black angora sweater, conscious of the fact she was braless underneath it because of her hurried dash to get dressed and answer the door. 'No. He hasn't. There wasn't a chance with the snow still lying so thick on the ground. Was there—was there a particular reason you dropped by?'

'There was, as a matter of fact. Mind if I come in for a minute?'

'I'm—I'm rather busy at the moment, as it happens.'

'Oh…' Clearly taken aback at having his plans thwarted, the farmer's son took a few seconds to reassemble his thoughts. 'I suppose I'll just have to say what I want to say out here, then.'

Stealing a furtive glance down the hall, Ailsa half expected to see Jake descending the staircase at the end of it. Thankfully, no such disturbing vision appeared. She returned her full attention to the man in front of her, noticing just then that his breath made little clouds of steam whenever it hit the frosted air. Feeling suddenly guilty at making him stand outside in such bitter weather, she opened the door wide, adding a cheery smile for good measure.

'On second thoughts, why don't you come into the warm for a minute? Go into the kitchen, I've just got to pop upstairs for something.'

As soon as a pleased Linus passed her in the hallway, Ailsa shut the door behind him and fled up the stairs. In the bedroom, now fully dressed, Jake was fastening his leather belt round his jeans. When he glanced up to acknowledge her return his accusing glare made her insides turn over.

'Why did you ask him in? I thought you were going to tell whoever it was that you were busy...*especially* him.'

'He came round to ask me something. I couldn't leave him shivering on the doorstep, for goodness' sake!'

'Does he always make such a nuisance of himself?' Jake scowled.

Hating the idea that he was disappointed in her because she hadn't put Linus off and returned to bed, Ailsa was also resentful that he seemed to be assuming some kind of right to say who she could or couldn't invite into her own home. 'He's not being a nuisance. I told you—he's a good neighbour and friend. The sooner I go downstairs and talk to him, the sooner he'll leave. I'm sure it won't take long. You can wait up here, if you like.'

Not waiting to hear his answer, she grabbed her bra off the silk eiderdown and, with her back to Jake, lifted her sweater over her head so that she could put it on. Before she had the chance to secure the front fastening he stepped up behind her and—*shockingly*—pushed the thin straps aside, cupping her breasts. Molten heat, want and need suffused her.

'Jake...*don't*!' But even as she instructed him in the negative her body and senses were silently pleading for more of the same. It took *Herculean* strength of mind to divert him. 'You mustn't... We mustn't... For goodness' sake, Linus is waiting downstairs!'

'Let him wait' His low-pitched growl was sexy and commanding as he caught an aching nipple between thumb and forefinger and pinched it.

Suppressing a groan, she grabbed onto her swiftly diminishing will with all her might, turning in his arms to chastise him. As soon as she did, her mouth was crushed relentlessly and passionately beneath his, his silken tongue hotly invading her so that they shared the same devastating breath. With a supreme effort Ailsa tore her lips away, holding onto his iron-hard shoulders because if she didn't her knees would crumple and she might well fall over. The warmly delicious scent of his body and teasing blue-eyed smile fired another devastating aside into senses that were already overwhelmed by him.

'You don't play fair.'

'Did I ever claim to? Sometimes a man has to use whatever advantage he can lay his hands on.'

'You've got to let me dress. The sooner I go downstairs and talk to him, the sooner he'll go. Then we can carry on talking. We were going to do that...remember?'

Sighing ruefully, Jake gently stroked back some drifting strands of her hair with his fingers. 'How can I deny you anything when you stand there looking at me with those big doe eyes—and half naked to boot?'

'It's not just the male sex that knows how to use the advantages in their armoury.' She smiled. Standing on tiptoe, Ailsa planted a brief affectionate kiss on his mouth, then firmly pushed him away. 'I won't be long,' she promised, finally able to fasten her bra and slip her sweater back on.

'You'd better not be.'

CHAPTER NINE

'SORRY to keep you waiting, Linus. Can I get you a cup of tea or coffee?'

'No, thanks. I can't stay very long, I'm afraid.'

Her neighbour's assertion was music to Ailsa's ears right then. But even as she sighed inwardly with relief, she didn't escape feeling guilty. He was standing in the middle of the kitchen, his shoulders hunched defensively, like a schoolboy about to confess some errant misdemeanour. She'd never seen him appear so ill at ease.

'All right, then. Would you like to sit down while we talk?'

Moving across to the kitchen table, she pulled out two chairs—one for her guest and one for herself. After that, apart from the hum of the radiator and the steady tick of the wall clock behind her, silence stretched out between them for what felt like a disconcertingly long time. Just when Ailsa wondered if he was ever going to sit down or speak at all, Linus dropped down into his chair and leant earnestly across the table.

'I was wondering what your plans were for Christmas Day?' His dark eyes anxiously roved her face. 'Only, if you're free, I was going to ask if you and Saskia would like to have lunch with me… That is…it won't be just me… unfortunately.' He grimaced. 'My father and uncle will

be there as well. To tell you the truth, we'd really appreciate some female company. An all-male household can get
a bit much sometimes.' A red flush tinged his weathered
cheeks for a moment.

Sheer surprise stunned Ailsa into silence. Of all the
things he might have been going to ask her, she definitely
hadn't expected an invitation to lunch on Christmas Day.
Staring at him blankly for a moment, she knew it was her
turn to swiftly reassemble her thoughts. 'It's very kind of
you to invite us, Linus, it really is… But I was actually
planning on just staying at home with Saskia. We've come
to regard the day as a special mother-and-daughter time.
We've been looking forward to it for months now.'

'Oh…'

'Linus…hello.'

The familiar smoky voice that sounded behind them
startled her. Her visitor seemed taken aback too—as if
Jake's sudden appearance had put him on edge.

'Hello,' he answered reluctantly.

Wishing that Jake had simply waited until Linus had
gone, Ailsa felt her gaze magnetised by him as he moved
to stand by her side, her heart racing as with a lazy little
smile he reached for her hand and raised it to his lips. The
provocative kiss he bestowed didn't just graze her knuck-
les, as she'd expected it to, but was deliberately planted in
the centre of her palm instead. Even though she knew the
gesture was probably designed to stake his claim in front
of the other man, it still made Ailsa tingle as if she'd received a mild electric shock.

'Am I interrupting something?' Jake asked smoothly.

Linus shook his head, his air that of a man who had just
been well and truly *crushed*. A wave of guilt rolled over
her.

'I was inviting Ailsa and her daughter to spend Christ-

mas Day with us, but she's told me they usually spend it
on their own.' The farmer pushed to his feet, the scarlet
flush beneath his skin that had appeared earlier returning
with a vengeance. His dark eyes moved from Ailsa to Jake,
then back to Ailsa again. 'I didn't realise that you and—'

'Jake.'

She registered the controlled politeness of her ex-husband's
voice, but knew instinctively that his tone might change to
a far less agreeable one should Linus be foolish enough to
challenge it. Thankfully…he *didn't*.

'You didn't realise what?' Jake pressed mildly.

'It doesn't matter.' The other man was already moving
towards the door. 'You're a very lucky man, if you don't
mind my saying so? Ailsa is one of the nicest people you
could wish to have for a neighbour, and her—your daughter—is charming.'

'I definitely have to agree with you on both counts.'

'You must be relieved that the snow is thawing at last,
so you can get to the airport and fly back to Copenhagen
in time for Christmas. It must be especially beautiful at
this time of year.'

'It is.'

'Well…I hope you enjoy the holiday when you get
there.'

'Thanks.' Jake's glance settled thoughtfully on Ailsa
for a moment, before moving back to Linus.

'I'll—I'll see you out.' Slipping into the hallway ahead
of her visitor, Ailsa almost held her breath all the way to
the front door. She couldn't help feeling as if she'd been
caught in the middle of a threatening storm. When the
rumbles died away, as they had now started to, her whole
body would be limp with relief. Her hand fumbled a little
with the heavy brass doorknob. As she exposed Linus and

herself to the raw wind blowing outside, she said, smiling, 'I really do appreciate your invitation, you know?'

Stopping thoughtfully beneath the peg-tiled porch, Linus turned round to survey her, 'Do you? I hope you don't think I was being a bit too presumptuous? I didn't realise that you and your ex were getting back together or I would never have asked.'

She supposed it was only natural, after Jake kissing her hand in front of him, that Linus would assume they were getting back together... She glanced awkwardly down at the ground. It wasn't as though she'd ever encouraged Linus in any way, yet she still felt uncomfortably as though she was deceiving him.

'I'm really sorry that I couldn't accept, but I hope you can still have a nice Christmas with your family.'

A drop of melting ice from the roof above him splashed down onto the dark curls that were slowly springing back into life after being so tidily combed down. Almost absent-mindedly, he patted it away. 'I expect it will be very much the same routine as other years. I'll still have to get up early to feed the animals and clean out the pens. My uncle will cook the dinner as he usually does—we're having a goose—and my father will drink a bit more malt whisky than is good for him. After that we'll watch some daft re-run on the television. Anyway, however you spend it, I hope that you will also enjoy the day. I expect we'll see each other at some point after the holiday?'

'Take care, Linus and—and thanks for all you've done for me and Saskia throughout the year.'

'It was my pleasure. Bye, now.'

Her chest tightened in sympathy as she watched him negotiate the now less than pristine snow on the path that led out from the stone-walled confines of the house. Waiting until he'd climbed into his tractor, she gave him a brief wave, then shut the door and returned inside.

'I told you he had more than just being a friendly neighbour on his mind.'

Turning round to face her from his stance in front of the window, Jake was unsmiling...*irritated*, Ailsa would have said.

'That's neither here nor there, and you know it!' Irritated or not, she wasn't going to put up with it. 'Why didn't you wait upstairs until he was gone, like I suggested?'

Raising a dark gold eyebrow, he scowled. 'Are you telling me that you would have accepted his invitation to lunch?'

'You heard him tell you I'd already declined as I'm spending Christmas Day on my own with Saskia.'

He exhaled a heavy sigh. 'Is that really what you want to do... Spend Christmas on your own with our daughter?'

'It's what I usually do...why?'

'I know I haven't got round to asking you yet, but the idea of you coming back and spending Christmas with me and Saskia in Copenhagen has been on my mind since I woke up this morning. That's why I got up early and went for a walk. I needed to think about plans. Plus I wanted to check out the state of the roads—see if we could make it to the airport either today or tomorrow. Preferably *today*... It's a good idea, when you come to think about it. That way you get to see our daughter much sooner, and you don't have to spend the season alone.'

'So you're feeling sorry for me now, are you?' she snapped, feeling inexplicably emotional.

'Sorry for you? If you think that's what's motivated me to ask you—*especially* after last night—then I'm honestly stunned.'

It had seriously upset Ailsa when Jake had shown up a

couple of days ago to tell her that Saskia would be extending her stay in Copenhagen. How could she have known that the situation would change so dramatically in so brief a time? That their enforced togetherness would stir up feelings that wouldn't easily be subdued and that she'd be deluged by taunting reminders of how good they had once been together? Now, because he had made that remark about leaving soon, she was privately climbing the walls at the reality of him not being around. That was why the idea of going to Denmark was more than tempting.

But, as much as her heart ached to be with him, and to see her precious child much sooner than she'd expected, how could she do it? How could she return there as if everything between them had been put right and there were no more problems? There was so much still to discuss, and she had no idea where any of it would lead when they did talk about it. She might have even made the situation *worse*, because now that she and Jake had been intimate again her heart was wide open to even more hurt.

He'd denied there was anyone else, but she couldn't be absolutely certain that he didn't have some woman waiting for him when he returned to the luxurious town house that was his home. If he did, no doubt she would be a much more glamorous and *worldly* woman than Ailsa. Perhaps she was one of those women he had mentioned who was of the opinion that his cruel scar gave him a certain 'piratical' appeal?

'Whatever you might think,' Jake said now, 'my intentions are good. To learn that Linus had invited you and Saskia to Christmas lunch made everything even clearer to me. I'm sure he's a decent guy, Ailsa, but I'm not going to give up the chance of you spending Christmas with me just because he's around. I *want* you to come back with me. I know that Saskia will be delighted if you do, and so will my mother. She often asks after you. Unfortunately, up until now, I haven't been able to tell her how you're doing. I really regret that we haven't talked since—since what happened.'

He was standing by the granite worktop and Ailsa saw his fingers visibly tighten round the rolled edge. They flexed so hard that they turned corpse-white. A cold chill ran down her spine. Then she was moving towards him, as if her body's volition had overridden her mind's, and she trembled with the force of the feelings that gripped her.

'We've become so good at not saying the right words, haven't we? At not calling a thing what it is? I know we talked about some important stuff at last, but we've skirted around the issues that really matter like they're unexploded bombs that might go off in our faces. Well, I've got news for you, Jake… The bombs have already exploded and we've caught the fall-out good and proper. When you say "what happened" you should say "when our baby was killed and the love we had for each other died too." Isn't that what you really mean to say?'

The blue eyes that lifted towards her were as desolate as the bleakest of winter nights. 'And that makes every-thing better, does it? Calling a thing what it is?'

She threw up her hands in near-despair. 'At least it's being real… At least it's the truth. I'm not saying I want to hang on to these feelings for ever—they've already cut my heart to shreds, so why would I? I don't want to add to my suffering, and I really do want to move on. For the past four years I've been stuck…*welded* in the mire of that terrible event. Trapped so deep in it that at times I've felt almost paralysed. I dread to think what that might have done to Saskia. She's so vibrant and alive, and I haven't been the mother I want to be for so long that I know that things have to change. They've *got* to change. What I'm telling you now, Jake, is that I want to speak my truth and then I want you to speak yours…to really tell me how you felt then and how you feel now. After that… Well, we'll see.'

'Then tell me, Ailsa. Tell me your truth and I'll listen. Then I'll tell you mine.'

Catching her by the hand, Jake stared hard at her slender, ringless fingers. As if disappointed by what he saw, he let it drop back down to her side again. She wondered if the pounding of her heart was as audible to him as it was to her just then.

'Very well, then… When I came to after the operation and they told me I'd lost the baby I thought I was in the middle of the most terrifying nightmare. I thought, *Any minute now I'll wake up and see that I'm at home in bed with Jake.* I thought…I thought I'd tell you about my horrific dream and you'd comfort me…lay your hand over my tummy, where our baby was still growing…still thriving… and say, *"See? It was only a dream, Ailsa. Everything is fine."'*

Her throat tightening unbearably, she threaded restless fingers through the long dark skeins of her hair. She hardly dared glance at Jake for fear she would come undone completely. 'But it wasn't a dream,' she continued huskily. 'And although they gave me morphine to dull the pain I still hurt. I hurt *beyond* any pain I'd ever experienced before. I'm not just talking about physical discomfort. I felt empty…empty and useless now that my baby was gone. Like a mere husk of the woman I used to be. They say that sometimes the bereaved are numb with grief, but I felt everything—as though my very skin was being flayed with knives. I mourned my child and then I mourned *us*, Jake. I mourned us because I knew it was the end even then. I thought things had been hard enough, but how could we ever get over that? How could we carry on and behave like normal civilised people?

'It wasn't long before we both realised that we couldn't. Our lives would never be "normal" again, and because of that we took all our rage and pain out on each other. I was glad when you asked me for a divorce. I mean it. I was glad that you would have the chance to rebuild your life with someone else—to father a baby with someone else. But when you left...' Lifting her head to face him squarely for the first time since she'd started speaking, Ailsa found it almost impossible to continue, because her throat swelled and ached so much. 'When you left...' With a little shake of her head she indicated she couldn't go on.

Jake's natural instinct was to haul her into his arms and hold her for the longest time. She looked ridiculously young and vulnerable with her chestnut hair framing the perfect pale oval of her face...like a child. But her raw admission of how she had felt at the time of their baby's death and then afterwards, when she'd believed that their love had died too, was like a small but devastating tsunami crashing inside him.

When the dust began to clear a little he had the peculiar sense of having missed something important...something *vital*. The realisation hit that he'd perhaps not been as aware of his good fortune as he should have been when they were married. Instead he had blithely greeted each day imagining that the comfortable existence they'd enjoyed could go on for ever, without anything too serious ever endangering it. Even the fact that he'd become a workaholic like his father. Foolishly, perhaps even *arrogantly*, he had cocooned himself from the remote and terrible possibility that everything he loved could be ripped from his arms in less than a blink of an eye... *He'd never even considered it.*

But then why should he have? His friends and colleagues had always told him that he had the Midas touch—that everything remotely associated with him effortlessly turned to gold. Jake had it all, they said—supportive parents, a fabulous career, wealth beyond most people's wildest dreams and then, if that wasn't enough, he had a beautiful wife and daughter as well. Up until that horrific day when that drunken driver had ploughed into his car he had seen no reason to dispute that gilt-edged belief. The very notion of such a cataclysmic event had truly been the stuff of nightmares...

His agitated gaze came to rest on the moist bronze-gold of Ailsa's bewitching eyes. 'I was like a sleepwalker,' he began. 'Not just after the accident, when life became a living nightmare, but before it too. I didn't notice enough of the things that were important to me. I was so fixated on the business that I missed the fact that I was lucky to have you in my life at all. It's a terrible thing to admit, but maybe I even took you for granted. My focus was all on my work—on wanting to prove to my father that I could be everything he wanted me to be and more. My great desire was to show him that when the time came for me to take over the business I could make it even more successful. I became so fixated on that goal that I didn't pay proper attention to my life...to *our* lives together. In the split second before that car hit us I didn't see my life flash before me, as people sometimes say they do. What I saw instead was that I was about to lose everything I loved *more* than life itself.'

Pausing to inhale a steadying breath, Jake absently touched his fingertips to the ridged contours of his scar. Noticing with a jolt that the tears in Ailsa's eyes were spilling over and sliding in an unchecked stream down her face, he pulled his hand away and, still agitated, tunnelled his fingers through his hair. It was perhaps the hardest thing he had ever done—to talk candidly like this. While the instinct to stop—to hide behind his defences as he had so often done in the past—surfaced again and again, he forced himself to stay strong and, as Ailsa had asked, to speak his truth.

'It brought me to my knees, losing our son. I could hardly believe that such a thing could happen to me…to *us*. And because I was hurting so bad I took it out on you, Ailsa. I meant to be a support to you, a comfort, but instead I effected an even greater distance between us than the one we'd been struggling with already. It was probably far crueller than the bitter words I sometimes threw at you. You were bitter with me too. The truth is it was our emotional *neglect* of each other that finally drove us apart, wasn't it? And, because *finally* I couldn't bear what was happening to our relationship, I knew I had to be the one to bring the misery to an end. The act was a double-edged sword. Yes, it freed us a little from our pain as a couple, but individually…it simply left us to endure it alone. Was that any better?' He stared hard at Ailsa. 'It certainly didn't feel like it to me. You asked me to tell you how I feel now? Well…to be honest, I'm still trying to figure that out. In the meantime, I'm simply grateful that we're talking again.'

'Thank you.'

Her words were so soft—softer than the delicate brush of a summer breeze against a voile curtain. Jake wondered if he'd imagined hearing them at all. But when he studied her face, she was scrubbing her tears away and smiling. Not comprehending, he stared at her. 'What for?'

'For telling me your truth.'

The doubt and fear inside him eased a little. 'You're welcome.' Closing his fist, he glanced it lightly against the smooth granite worktop beside him. 'Are we done now?'

'If you mean am I going to raise the topic again while we're together, then, no. I'm not. I've realised that to keep going over the pain of the past can make for a very sad existence. Well, I don't just want to *exist*, Jake. I want to live…properly and fully. Today is a new day…a clean page that has yet to be written on. From now on I want to treat every day like that. I want to believe in the possibility of being happy again.'

'So…will this new affirmation have any bearing on your decision to come to Copenhagen with me?' he asked, his lips wrestling with the surprising desire to smile too.

'I think it will…yes.' She hugged her arms over the black sweater that Jake was suddenly jealous of, because of its intimate proximity to her lovely body.

'And your decision is…?'

'I think I *will* take the opportunity to go back with you—to see Saskia and to meet up with your mother again. I'd like to tell her personally how sorry I was to hear about your dad's passing, and that I'll always remember him. But, Jake…?'

'Yes?'

'Just because we've been honest with each other at last it doesn't mean that we're making any promises about the future, does it?'

Feeling his heart miss a beat, like a hurdler who had miscalculated the distance to the next hurdle, knowing his mistake had cost him the race, he forced another smile to his lips. 'No. It doesn't. Like you, all I want to do now is to take one day at a time.'

'Okay. I suppose I'd better cook us some breakfast and then tidy up the house a bit, in case we have to leave soon.'

'It might be a good idea if you packed too.'

'I was just coming round to that, but— Oh! I've just thought of another thing.'

Watching her tap her fingers against her adorable chin, Jake smiled benevolently. 'What's that?'

'Saskia's Christmas presents. I mean, I still have some to get, but I've got quite a few that are already wrapped. Can I bring them with us?'

'Maybe a couple of small things—but you're going to have ample opportunity to visit the Christmas markets and get some more. At any rate, she won't lack for gifts on Christmas Eve…not if her grandmother has anything to do with it!'

Ailsa's animated face told Jake she'd just remembered something else. 'Didn't you say that she'd given you a letter to bring with you that had a list of things she might like in it?'

With a stab of guilt, he remembered the envelope he'd hastily thrown into his overnight bag when he'd left Copenhagen. 'She did. Why don't we read it when we get home? We're not going to be able to shop here if we want to leave today.'

'You're right. Well, I suppose before I do anything else I'd better go and pack…just in case. Do you think we *can* get a flight today?'

'If the planes are flying out of Heathrow I don't doubt it. I'll make some calls in a minute.'

'What about the roads? Do you think they'll be clear enough for us to get to the airport?'

'I'd forgotten how much you worry. Trust me, sweetheart… If I say we'll get there and everything will be all right, then it will.'

Colouring, she tucked a long strand of silky chestnut hair behind her ear and shrugged. 'Okay, I believe you. One more thing… Where will I be staying? At your mother's with Saskia? Or—or…?' She coloured again, this time a deep shade of russet-pink.

'I thought that you could stay with me.' Unable to help it, Jake inserted a hint of steel into his tone. 'I'll probably have to work up until Christmas Eve, but I'll make sure that Alain is at your disposal for whenever you want to visit Saskia at my mother's or go shopping. I imagine we'll all spend Christmas Day with my mother. How do you feel about that?' His gut felt as if it was clamped in a steel vice as he waited apprehensively for her answer.

'That sounds fine. Will you ring Saskia and let her know that we're coming?'

'I'll ring as soon as I've booked our flight.'

'Good.'

Ailsa left him alone then. For a long time Jake just stood staring out of the window at the melting snow, the lingering scent of her perfume tying his insides into knots as he fought to get his churning emotions under control....

CHAPTER TEN

WITH the usual commanding ease with which he was able to make most things happen, Jake got them an afternoon flight out of Heathrow that day. By the time Alain had picked them up from Kastrup Copenhagen airport at the other end and driven them to Jake's five-storey house at one of the wealthiest addresses in the city it was getting on towards eleven in the evening.

Having spoken to her daughter a couple of times before and after the first-class flight from Heathrow, Ailsa could hardly wait to see her again. Even though their reunion would have to wait until tomorrow, because they had arrived so late, she didn't forget that it was thanks to her ex-husband that they would be meeting up much sooner than she'd expected. It was a precious gift she wouldn't take for granted.

Throughout the seamless journey, Jake had been unusually quiet. Ailsa was hardly surprised when she recalled the depth and frankness of his reflections about the tragedy that had driven them apart. That would be apt to leave the strongest person emotionally drained. And, because she was mindful of the deeply emotional places they had both visited over the past few days, she'd chosen not to disturb his reverie by talking. In fact, apart from eating lunch, she had slept for most of the flight. When she'd woken,

she hadn't told him that she'd been dreaming about him...
dreaming about the exotic honeymoon they'd shared in the
Caribbean island of St. Kitts after their wedding.

Although they'd been in one of the most beautiful loca-
tions for a honeymoon in the world, surrounded by tropical
forest and a sapphire-blue sea, they had hardly ventured
out from their luxurious villa. Apart from a welcome dip
or two in the jewel-like warm sea, and enjoying first-class
cuisine prepared by their chef out on the patio, their long
hot days had mostly been languorously viewed from their
opulent bed through the open French doors. The erotic
memory of that time still had the power to flood her body
with heat and make her tingle.

'Home sweet home,' Jake drawled now, bringing Ailsa
sharply back to the present.

Just as her ex-husband had only set eyes on her traditional English country cottage for the first time a short
while ago, it was now Ailsa's turn to reciprocate and experience for the first time the opulent modernity of his
own elite abode. For a girl who had been raised in a very
basically furnished children's home with minimal creature
comforts the sense of wealth and exclusivity that reached
out to embrace her as she stepped into the white marble
hallway quickly reminded her of the stark differences in
her and Jake's backgrounds. Even though she was well
acquainted with the rich trappings of the Larsen family's
wealth, it still took her aback to experience it first-hand.
Her gaze sweeping the 'winter palace' furnishings, and
the very contemporary modern art that Jake had always
had a strong preference for on the walls, she suddenly had
the sense of being ridiculously shy and ill-prepared here
on his home turf.

'It's very beautiful,' she murmured quietly, slipping off
her leather gloves.

'I say home, but you understand that I use the term loosely?' With a wry smile, he stepped towards her. 'Are you hungry?'

'I had a meal on the plane, remember?'

'That was hours ago.'

'Are *you* hungry, Jake?' Unthinkingly, Ailsa batted the question back at him. It was only when she saw his arresting eyes darken to a sultry navy blue that she realised how it had affected him.

'For food? No. But if you're asking if I'm hungry for you, Ailsa, then the answer will always be yes.'

Lightly touching her hair, he gave her a smile that was tender rather than passionate, but it still had the effect of quickening her pulse and warming her heart as if she'd just imbibed the most intoxicating brandy.

'Would you mind if I freshened up? You know what it's like after making a journey...even a first-class one... you can feel quite washed out.' Awkwardly, hardly even knowing if the words that spilled out of her mouth made any sense at all because of Jake's disturbing proximity, she smoothed her hand down over the lapels of her long camel-coloured coat and moved towards the familiar tote Alain had left standing alongside her suitcase on the marble floor.

'I asked my housekeeper Magdalena to prepare a room for you,' he declared, stopping her in her tracks. 'I'll show you where it is.'

Why did he appear to be deliberately avoiding her gaze as he made this statement? Ailsa wondered. A pang of disquiet coiled in the pit of her stomach.

As if intuiting her confusion, he exhaled a deep sigh. 'I didn't want to presume that you'd want to share my room...plus, I thought you'd like a little privacy to gather your thoughts. Anyway, let me take that for you.'

Carrying her tote as well as her suitcase, Jake led her up the gracefully curving staircase, and as she followed him, silently admiring the impressive width of his shoulders beneath his coat and the straight dark gold hair that grazed his collar, she hoped he was being honest about the reason he was giving her a room of her own. Her insides boomeranged at the idea it might be because some other woman had recently shared his bed and perhaps had left some of her belongings there. *After the intimacy they had shared at the cottage, just the thought of such a possibility made her feel ill.*

As she'd anticipated, the room he showed her into was furnished in a very clean, 'no frills' elegant Scandinavian style. The furnishings were all painted in antique white and had a very appealing faded charm—*shabby chic*, as some designers called it. The ambience was restful and inviting, and definitely peaceful. Ailsa loved it straight away. Although, when her glance came to rest on the double bed, with its curved headboard inlaid with delicate floral marquetry, her heart skipped a regretful beat. Yes, it looked inviting and restful, but without Jake beside her she knew it would be a lonely experience sleeping there on her own.

'The bathroom is just through here.' He opened another door to reveal a dazzling *en-suite*, giving Ailsa a glimpse of graceful pine and polished stainless steel.

She smiled, wishing she didn't feel so deeply disappointed at not being invited to share *his* room. If he was always hungry for her, as he'd asserted, then why hadn't he asked her?

Moving to the doorway that led back onto the hall landing, he glanced down at his watch. 'It's very late. I think I'll turn in too. In the morning, over breakfast, we can discuss when we're visiting Saskia.'

'I'd like to go as early as possible, if that's okay?'

'That's fine with me.'

'Jake?'

'What is it?'

'We didn't look at the letter she gave you—the one with her Christmas list in. I'd like us to glance over it together before we leave for your mother's house.'

'No problem.'

The smile he returned in answer to this request was brief and disappeared far too quickly—like a glimpse of sunlight that she wished would stay on a day that was grey and unpromising. One minute it gave her hope for better times to come, then in the next the clouds reappeared to cover it, leaving the day *and* the spirits gloomy again.

'Goodnight, Ailsa. Sleep well, huh?'

The door clicked shut even as she murmured, 'Goodnight. I hope you sleep well too.'

Going downstairs to find her way to the kitchen the next morning, Ailsa was greeted by Jake's housekeeper, Magdalena. The woman was probably in her mid to late forties, had a crisply cut white-blond bob, and was tall and slim. Her eyes were as grey as an icy lake, but somehow managed to reflect genuine warmth despite their glacial hue. She was definitely a far cry from the plump and grandmotherly Rose, who had been their part-time housekeeper when Ailsa and Jake had lived in London.

'*God morgen.* You must be Ailsa. I am so pleased to meet you at last.'

The woman greeted her as if she truly *was* pleased, and Ailsa's small hand was soon engulfed by the blonde's slender larger one. 'And you must be Magdalena. I'm very pleased to meet you too.' She smiled back.

'I can now see where your lovely daughter gets her

beauty from. What amazing hair you have, if you don't
mind my saying so.'

Alisa had sat in front of the dressing table mirror that
morning and brushed out all the snags and tangles that
had accumulated on her travels yesterday, as if psycho-
logically she needed a bit of a boost to face the day. If she
also wanted to look her best for the man who had once
been her husband, then Ailsa kept that disturbing realisation to herself. Even though she'd slept surprisingly well,
she was still smarting a little at Jake giving her a room of
her own rather than inviting her to share his.

'Thank you,' she murmured in reply to the housekeeper's compliment.

'Why don't you sit down at the breakfast table and I
will get you a hot drink?' Magdalena suggested.

'A cup of tea would be great…thanks.' Ailsa moved
across to the rectangular pine table that was positioned opposite French windows overlooking a narrow but long garden. She shook her head with wry humour when she saw
the light snowflakes that were tumbling from the skies.
Already they were rendering the immaculate lawn lacy
white.

Seeing the interested direction of her glance, the Danish housekeeper shrugged and smiled. 'Most of the snow
we have had over the last few days melted away yesterday. Today, when you and Mr Larsen are home, it returns!
Little Saskia will be so pleased, yes?'

'She'll be overjoyed. I think she's been praying for a
white Christmas all year. By the way, do you know if
Jake—if Mr Larsen is up yet?'

'Goodness me, he got up hours ago! I made him a good
breakfast and afterwards he went straight to his study to
work. Your husband is a very early riser and he works so
hard… He puts us all to shame.'

'He's not my hus—'

Ailsa's pained admission that she and Jake weren't married any more was prevented by Magdalena's cheery, 'My own husband Kaleb admires him greatly. Even though Kaleb is not as experienced as some of Larsen's staff, he would work day and night for your husband—I know it.' The cheery smile suddenly vanished, to be replaced by a soft, thoughtful frown. 'He gave him a chance when no one else would even think of it. Kaleb was an alcoholic, you see,' she explained. 'He lost his brother after he'd helped take care of him through a long and crippling illness and it went downhill from there. He just lost the belief that anything mattered any more and started to drink. We—we had parted, and he was sleeping rough, living on the streets. Mr Larsen stopped to talk to him one evening, outside a conference centre where the company had been holding a meeting, and spoke to him for a long time. Yes... Mr Larsen helped him believe in himself again. When Kaleb and I got back together, he offered me this job as his housekeeper. I was working for a hotel chain before this, but I wasn't happy there. Forgive me—I am talking far too much and you are probably longing for your cup of tea and some breakfast, yes?'

'Please don't apologise.' Moved that this woman had shared her personal story of hardship and sadness with her, Ailsa felt her spirits lift at hearing of Jake's great kindness to her and her husband. 'I'm very glad that you shared this with me, Magdalena. Thank you.'

'And I am glad that you do not mind me telling you about Kaleb and me. Now I will get you that cup of tea!'

'Thank you.'

'And, after I make the tea, what would you like for breakfast?'

The woman was already at the streamlined stainless

steel cooker, placing a copper kettle onto a burner to boil.
For a few uncertain moments Ailsa stared at the back of
her precision-cut bob and neatly dressed figure, in an un-
fussy ecru sweater and slim black skirt, and wondered
how someone so obviously efficient and in such clear ad-
miration of her boss's work ethic and personal kindness
would receive a request for just a slice of toast. She definitely got the feeling that 'a good breakfast' round here
meant something a bit more substantial than that.

A much more appealing if *risky* idea slid into her mind.
Already having located the state-of-the-art coffee machine,
she moved towards it, reaching up to the pine shelving
above, where the pristine white crockery was uniformly
displayed, for a single cup and saucer. 'I'd like to take a
cup of coffee to Mr Larsen. Can you show me how this
machine works, Magdalena?'

'Of course.' The older woman smiled approvingly. 'It
will be my pleasure.'

Finishing his umpteenth call to the office that morning, Jake threw his mobile phone down onto the satin-
wood desk, then leaned wearily back in his chair. Several
thoughts jockeyed for precedence in his brain all at once.
One fact was indisputable. He desperately needed some
air to clear his head.

Glancing through the panoramic window in front of
him, to see the flurry of snowflakes that were drifting
down, he hoped the snow wouldn't settle too deep—at
least not until they had driven safely to his mother's house
in the country. Was Ailsa up yet? Had she slept at all last
night? *God knows, he hadn't!* He'd swear he'd barely shut
his eyes for even a minute. How was he supposed to sleep
when his body was gripped with a fever of need to hold

her, to make love to her, to hear her whimper and moan
his name out loud when she came?

He loosed a heartfelt curse under his breath. Had he
imagined that her beautiful amber eyes had reflected
disappointment when he'd shown her into her room last
night? A room that she would sleep in *alone*? Still privately
stunned that she'd agreed to come back to Denmark with
him, Jake hadn't wanted to push his luck by assuming she
would continue to want to sleep with him. Common sense
told him to tread carefully, even when his heart ached for
him to risk everything. If he was too eager, too desperate,
he reasoned it might just as likely drive Ailsa away. The
last thing he wanted was to make her feel trapped.

Head in his hands, he let another groan escape him. It
was a double-edged sword, he knew, but he could really
use some more coffee to clear his thumping head and help
him think straight!

Right on cue, there was a knock at the door. 'Magdalena, you must be a mind-reader.' He sat up straight, then
swivelled round in the leather office chair that was on
casters. At the unexpected sight of his svelte ex-wife in
slim black cords and a pink V-necked sweater, her glorious chestnut hair flowing down over her shoulders to her
hips, Jake stared in mute surprise. She was bearing a small
tray with a single cup of coffee on it.

'It's me…not Magdalena.'

She threw him a smile that was naturally sweetly self-
conscious—the sight of which made the blood thicken and
slow in his veins. 'So I see,' he drawled.

'I thought you might like some coffee?'

'Coffee is always welcome…thanks.'

Moving towards the desk, Ailsa set down the tray beside
Jake's blotter. As she did so, his senses were held in thrall
by the hypnotic scent of perfume and warmly beguiling

woman. 'There you are,' she murmured, straightening to glance down at him.

'And here *you* are,' Jake answered, low-voiced, anchoring his palms either side of her slimly curvaceous hips and pulling her down onto his lap.

Even as her amber eyes rounded with shock his lips hungrily sought hers, and all thought of needing something to clear his head so that he could think straight went out of the window. When he was with this woman—this beguiling, intoxicating woman—he didn't *need* to think. Not when all he wanted to do was to *feel*, to experience every glorious sensation, every touch of her arresting body right down to the very depths of his innermost being—just as though it was the purest, sweetest oxygen he could ever breathe.

As he curved his hand round the back of her neck to deepen the searching, ravenous kiss he intended on continuing for a long, long time, her freshly shampooed hair glanced warmly against his jaw, curtaining them both from the rest of the world. Gliding his tongue into the hot satin interior of Ailsa's mouth was akin to submerging himself in the sweetest wild honey. When he felt her shapely bottom wriggle against his groin as she attempted to break off the feverish coupling of their lips, erotic near-*scalding* heat mercilessly hardened him.

Cupping her face, he made a sound that was half aroused groan, half dismayed protest at her calling a halt to the mindless pleasure he ached to prolong. 'Have you any idea what you do to me?' he husked.

'I—if I have such an effect on you—an effect we both don't seem able to fight—why didn't you invite me to stay with you last night instead of giving me a room on my own?'

A faint bloom of dusky pink seeped into her cheeks as

she posed the question, as if her own need embarrassed her. With his heartbeat thundering in his chest, Jake reached up to press the pad of his thumb almost fiercely across the exquisitely shaped mouth he could never seem to get enough of.

'Did you want me to invite you to share my bed, Ailsa?' he asked, gravel-voiced.

'How do you expect me to know anything when you look at me like that?' Clearly flustered, she sprang off of his lap to create a distance of several feet between them.

Jake got to his feet with a sigh that was part satisfaction and a whole lot frustration. 'Like what? How am I looking at you? Why don't you tell me, hmm?'

'Like—like…' She was coiling her hair round her ear, and even from a distance he could see that she trembled. 'Like you want to eat me!' she burst out, then spun away as if it was almost too much a test of endurance to stay facing him.

Chuckling, he dropped his hands to his jeans-clad hips. 'What if I do? What if I want to touch you—to kiss you everywhere—to make your heart pound and your blood turn to fire? Would you let me, Ailsa?'

Slowly, as if helplessly fascinated, she turned back. 'This is ridiculous. I only—I only came in here to bring you a cup of coffee.'

'Why didn't you just let Magdalena bring it?'

'Because I…' Her straight white teeth visited some unfair punishment on her plump lower lip. 'Because I wanted to know if the reason you didn't invite me to share your bed last night was because another woman had recently shared it with you!'

Jake walked slowly across the carpeted pine floor to plant himself in front of her. 'Do you really believe that? The only reason I didn't ask you to sleep with me last night was consideration for how you might be feeling. We'd had a long day's travelling and you looked tired. I thought you'd have more rest in a bed of your own. It was simply that, Ailsa.'

'Even so…you said—that is you told me that you don't live like a monk, or words to that effect. You're perfectly entitled, of course—to sleep with another woman, I mean. I haven't forgotten we've been divorced for quite some time. But still I…I hoped… Oh, never mind. I hardly even know what I'm saying. The whole situation is just too crazy for words.' She dropped her head to stare down at the floor.

With firm fingers, Jake raised her chin. Her beautiful amber eyes were a little moist, he saw. 'Just so that you know…I've never brought a woman back home with me here to share my bed. When I've been with someone— and it's only ever been purely for sex—I've taken her to a discreetly located hotel somewhere. The last time I was with a woman like that was about six months ago… okay?'

No, it's not okay! Ailsa wanted to yell at him and then thump his chest. Her reaction was crazy, possessive and jealous, and she hardly knew what to do with the pain her feelings wrought inside her. She loved him. He had equally endured the devastating hurt of losing their baby, even if they hadn't been able to stay together at the time, and she would *always* love him. For her, there was simply no other man nor ever would be. Jake was the father of their precious daughter and that counted for more than she could say. But even in the midst of her distress she knew it was hardly fair of her to expect him to have remained celibate for four long years.

She drew in a steadying breath and, stepping away from the touch that did indeed set her blood on fire, she made herself nod. 'Okay. When you've finished working, do you think we can discuss when we're going to see Saskia? Only the snow seems to be getting heavier, and we don't want to leave it too late to travel.'

He smiled at her then, and his haunting eyes had never seemed more heavenly blue. 'We'll go just as soon as I've finished my coffee...happy now?'

'Yes.' Crossing her arms over her dusky pink sweater, Ailsa moved across to the door. 'I'm happy. I'll just go to my room and get myself ready.'

'Ailsa?'

'Yes?'

'When we get back later on this evening, perhaps you'd like to move your things into my room?'

Swallowing down the egg-sized lump in her throat, she shrugged and murmured softly, 'Okay...'

It was unfortunate, Jake told her, but he had to look over some documents as they travelled out of the city into the Danish countryside. Ailsa smiled at him, knowing that because of the past it made him feel uncomfortable to tell her that, and saw he clearly regretted having to work instead of relaxing with her. The quiet, silver-haired Alain was driving them, and they both made themselves comfortable in the luxurious heated seats in the back—Jake to work and Ailsa to enjoy the sights and scenery as they travelled, and also to anticipate the joy of being reunited with their little girl.

Thinking about Saskia jogged her memory about something important. She turned to the preoccupied, darkly attired man sitting next to her, knowing she wouldn't think of disturbing him at all but for this one vital thing. His gaze was clearly absorbed in what he was reading, and there was a small but distinct frown between his dark gold brows as if what he read perturbed him in some way. Every now and then his pen scratched out several lines from the printed document resting on his lap.

'Jake?'

'Hmm?' He didn't even glance round.

'Did you bring Saskia's letter? I'd like to have a look at it if you did.'

'Saskia's letter?' As if snapping out of a trance, he refocused his compelling blue eyes to study Ailsa. 'Of course…it's right here.' Opening the tan leather attaché case that was positioned across his thighs, so he could rest his document on it as he wrote, he extracted a slim, slightly crumpled white envelope. He handed it to her with a grimace. 'I should have looked at it earlier with you, I know. I'm afraid that work got in the way this morning.'

'Never mind.' She gave him what she hoped was a reassuring smile. 'I'll look over the list and tell you what she wants, okay?'

'Good idea.' About to return to his paperwork, Jake paused. 'I'm giving my attention to this now so that I can take a few more days off than I'd anticipated taking. I'll probably finish up tomorrow…just so that you know.'

A flood of warmth poured into her belly. 'Thanks for telling me.'

Sitting back in her seat, Ailsa started to tear open the envelope. To her surprise, there were *two* neatly folded sheets of cream vellum. Grinning at the idea that Saskia's Christmas list was longer than her parents had anticipated, she carefully studied the first sheet of paper. The sight of the familiar childish handwriting in blue coloured pencil stung her eyes. Discreetly wiping them, so that Jake wouldn't see, she read the short, succinct request for presents that her daughter had written. As she'd expected, the requests were endearingly modest. In her mind, Ailsa added a few

ideas of her own. When she turned to the next sheet of
paper, what was written on it made her catch her breath.

> Dear Mama and Papa
> I don't mind if Father Christmas doesn't bring me
> anything on my other list. The present I would like
> most of all is for you two to get back together. It's
> very sad that my baby brother died and I never got to
> meet him, but I really want us to be a proper family
> again, with you both living at home with me.
> All my love, Saskia
> XXX

Biting her lip, Ailsa returned the first sheet of paper
to the crumpled envelope and surreptitiously slipped its
companion into the pocket of her wool jacket.

'Can I see?'

Jake's request jolted her.

'Of course.' Trying her best to stay calm, not to betray
the stormy feelings that were crashing through her, Ailsa
handed him the envelope. Turning her head, she stared out
of the window. Scenery flashed by in a blur of trees and
tarmac.

*Now wasn't the right time to share with him what was
so poignantly written on that second sheet of paper, she
decided, Even if her heart leapt with hope at the very idea
of fulfilling their daughter's wish.* It would be a grave mistake to presume anything about the future, to pressure him
in any way.

Helplessly glancing at his preoccupied chiselled profile
as he smilingly read his little girl's list, she let her gaze fall
upon his scar. Not for the first time her stomach clenched
with remembered sorrow at how he had come by it. She
made herself breathe out slowly. He needed time to get

to know her again, she thought. She wouldn't show him Saskia's request until he was ready. Jake needed to see that Ailsa had sincerely let go of any grudges from the past—that she forgave him for any of his own transgressions. She had meant it when she'd declared she wanted to move forward in life with a lot more optimism and faith. She kept it to herself that she hoped ultimately that it would be with *him*.

Serious doubt washed over her as she silently came to such a momentous conclusion. She might be willing to try again to make their relationship work, but could Jake tie himself to a woman who had no prospect of ever bearing the son he craved? Shutting her eyes for a long moment, she prayed that he wouldn't see it as the most awful negative. Most of all she wanted him to know that her love for him was strong and true, and that if he agreed to be with her again she would never again allow him to doubt it....

CHAPTER ELEVEN

THE stunning white house appeared in a wooded clearing at the end of a winding and narrow country road. Its impact was picturesque and magical. Bathed as it was in the familiar blue light common to this part of Europe, its enchanting impression was emphasised even more by the flurry of frozen white drifting steadily down from the sky.

But, however beautiful it was, Ailsa's attention wasn't absorbed by the house for long. For standing on the wooden steps that swept down to the curving gravel drive was a small girl dressed in jeans, a long hand-knitted pink cardigan, and a pair of light brown sheepskin-lined fur boots. She was out of the car and running towards the child before the ever-dutiful Alain could get to the passenger door to do the usual honours his job as chauffeur entailed.

'Mama!' Calling out to her in delight, Saskia hurried down the steps with her arms held wide.

Raining kisses down on the small blond head the minute they were reunited, Ailsa hugged her daughter tight, her heart pounding with joy and her senses breathing in her longed-for scent even as she sent up a fervent prayer of thanks. 'My goodness, I think you've grown! What on earth has Grandma been feeding you to help you get so tall?'

'I've been eating lots of home-made soup and potatoes.

It's so lovely to see you, Mama.' The big china-blue eyes so reminiscent of her handsome father's sparkled with happiness.

'It's lovely to see you too, baby. I've missed you so much.'

'And it's snowing too! I prayed and prayed for a white Christmas and my prayers have been answered.' The little girl glanced up at the sky in wonder.

'We've had lots of snow back home too.'

'Did you and Papa build a snowman?'

Ailsa flushed almost guiltily. 'No, darling, we didn't. I'm afraid it was so cold we were too busy just keeping warm.'

'Hello scamp.'

Jake reached them just as she finished speaking. Now it was his turn to bestow upon Saskia a loving embrace and to smother his child in warmly affectionate kisses. Still keeping hold of his daughter's small hand, over her head his smiling gaze fell into Ailsa's. A lock of tarnished gold hair had tumbled onto his still unlined brow, and it made her hand itch to sweep it back for him. She almost didn't breathe at the unrestrained look of pleasure and satisfaction so evident in his eyes. It struck her forcibly how different he appeared when he was truly happy and not weighed down with grief and regret. *How she had missed seeing him like that.*

'Let's go inside, shall we?' He started to walk up the steps with Saskia, then stopped to glance round at Ailsa. 'Come on, slowcoach… No doubt my mother's busy in the kitchen. She's been looking forward to seeing you again, Ailsa.'

'Has she?' It was hard to keep the doubt from her voice. What must Tilda Larsen think of her, making herself so distant from her son these past few years? Was she perhaps angry that her ex-daughter-in-law had all but cut him out of her life so thoroughly that she'd scarcely even had a conversation with him, even on the telephone? Ailsa could easily see that Jake's mother might feel aggrieved about that.

'Of course she has. Come on. It's cold out here.'

'What about Alain?' She swung round at the same time as the luxurious car started to reverse and pull out of the drive.

'He's going into the city on an errand for me. Don't worry—he'll be back later to take us home.'

'Grandma, they're here! Mama and Papa are here!'

Their daughter let go of Jake's hand and bounded ahead into the house in search of her grandmother. As soon as they stepped over the threshold Ailsa's senses were sub-merged in comforting warmth and good smells. She'd visited the Larsen family house many times during her marriage to Jake, and was no less enchanted now by the bright open spaces of the interior, with its blond wood floors, high ceilings and panoramic windows that let in every bit of light available—essential when the days were as short as they were in the wintertime.

After they'd both removed their shoes and hung up their jackets, with his hand placed lightly at her back Jake led Ailsa into the large bespoke kitchen—handmade by a local cabinet-maker when he was a teenager, he'd once told her. The petite, fair-haired woman holding out her arms to them both while Saskia hovered eagerly by her side hardly looked a day older than when Ailsa had last set eyes on her over four years ago. Yes, there were a few more threads of elegant silver weaving through her shoulder-length hair, but her lovely face was as warm and full of life as ever.

Waiting for the couple to reach her, she embraced Jake first of all, murmuring softly, 'My beautiful, beautiful son…' Her still stunning blue eyes lovingly drank him in, as though she would never be able to get enough of the sight of him.

Her throat tight, Ailsa forced a wobbly smile to her lips as Tilda turned her attention to her.

'Welcome home, Ailsa…my beloved *daughter*.'

It was that one simple word that broke the dam that was already pressing so impossibly behind her lids. Unable to curtail her emotion, she hugged the older woman as affectionately hard as she was being hugged, her fingers pressing into the soft black jersey of her dress with perhaps the greatest need for love and acceptance that she had ever experienced before. As if intuiting this, Tilda held her fast, her hand tenderly patting her back. Then, moving her hands to Ailsa's shoulders, she gently manouvered her to stand in front of her. The infinitely kind blue glance gently examined her face.

'Your heart has been darkened by sorrow for too long, my angel. It must be the worst pain of all for a mother to lose a child. I feel for you *and* for my dear son. I too have known sorrow since losing my Jacob. But our dear ones will not rest peacefully if we spend the rest of our lives in grief. They would want us to live, Ailsa…to live and to love and enjoy the time we have left, no?'

'You're right.' She sniffed, wiping her tears away with the tips of her fingers. 'Of course you're right. I was *so* sorry to hear about Jacob. I know how devoted you were to each other.'

'It has been hard without him, but every day gets a little easier if I can learn to be at peace—to accept rather than fight what has happened. Having my darling Saskia with me has helped me more than I can say, Ailsa. I thank you for agreeing to let her stay a bit longer with me. Now, Jake, why don't you take Ailsa into the living room and warm yourselves by the fire? Saskia and I will make you both a hot drink. Later we will have a late lunch of *steggt flaesk*.'

In the fading light of the afternoon and with the red and orange glow from the fire crackling in the grate, the elegant Christmas tree positioned just to the side of the wide picture windows wore a gentle cloak of illumination even without the benefit of the small white lights coiling through its branches. At the tip of the topmost branch re-sided a large gold star, and the rest of the tall spruce was dressed with a charming mix of traditional and home-made decorations.

The sight of it warmed every corner of Ailsa's heart. When she'd been in the children's home she'd used to dream of a home like this—a home where every impor-tant tradition was lovingly and joyfully celebrated. She glanced up. Hanging from the ceiling rose was a traditional Advent wreath, with its four red and white candles—one lit on each of the four Sundays leading up to Christmas Eve. She remembered being completely charmed by it when she'd first heard of the ritual.

Jake lightly caught her hand and led her to the invit-ingly comfortable sofa nearest to the fire. 'Are you okay?' he asked, concerned.

'I'm fine. It was quite emotional for me to have your mother greet me as warmly as that.'

'Why? Did you expect her not to?'

Discomfited, Ailsa lightly shrugged her shoulders. 'She hasn't seen me for over four years…I've barely spoken to her. I thought she might be angry that I haven't commu-nicated very much with you either.'

'If you expected her to be angry then you don't know her very well at all.'

Ailsa stayed silent. What could she say when all Jake had done was speak the truth? It made her realise that she'd become very good at keeping the people who had been the closest to her at arm's length. She prayed she'd never employed that tactic with her little girl and never *would*.

'Hey...' His fingertips grazed the side of her face and the edges of his sculpted lips lifted to form a smile. 'It's good to have you here, Ailsa...really good. It's been a long time.'

In his mind, Jake added, *It's good to have you back where you belong...back with the people who really care about you.* He'd often observed over the years they'd been together that sometimes she looked like a lost little girl. A far-away unhappy look would creep into her amber gaze, telling him that she was lost in the past—in the insecure, uncertain world of her childhood. His mother—his father too, in his own gruff way—had given him unstinting care and support throughout his life, and he couldn't begin to imagine how it must have been for Ailsa to have no one there for her except the staff at the children's home where she'd been raised.

When he'd fallen in love with her, vowing to marry her just as soon as it could be arranged—*yesterday* hadn't been nearly soon enough—he had promised himself that she would never again have to doubt that she was loved and cared for. *But when she'd lost their son, Jake had seemingly forgotten that promise.* He'd been so wrapped up in his own misery and grief that he'd somehow neglected to convey that one day everything would be all right again... that he would love her until the end of his days come what may. That the fact she could never again have children would not mar their happiness. He should have reassured her that he was totally happy with the precious little family he was already blessed with, and needed nothing else to complete his quota of joy. *But he hadn't reassured her.*

Instead he had walked away from their marriage to try and escape his own unbearable hurt.

'Papa, Grandma has helped me make some coffee for you and some tea for Mama, and we made these biscuits together too. But Grandma said to tell you that you mustn't eat too many or else you won't eat your lunch.'

'How am I supposed to resist them when you've made them look so tempting?' Jake grinned, helping himself to a slim piece of shortbread along with his cup of coffee.

Saskia held the tray towards her mother. 'Shall I take that for you, sweetheart?' Ailsa offered, smiling. 'It looks heavy.'

'I can manage. I'm getting very good at helping round the home—aren't I, Grandma?' The child saw that Tilda had entered the room and come to stand beside her.

'You are a constant surprise and wonder to me, *min skat.*'

'And now that you've served us our drinks, my angel, let me put that down for you.' Leaving his coffee on the small table beside the sofa, Jake relieved his daughter of the tray and set it down on the floor by his feet.

'Jake? Saskia has made some more shortbread that has yet to come out of the oven. Would you mind going into the kitchen with her and taking it out? While you do that, I will stay here and talk to Ailsa.'

Jake knew a moment's anxiety that his mother wanted to talk privately with Ailsa, but because he didn't have a chance to quiz her about it he had to trust that it wasn't going to be anything upsetting.

'No problem. Come on, sweetheart, we'll go and rescue your cookies from the oven before they burn to a crisp!'

Saskia pouted indignantly. 'They won't burn, Papa, be-cause Grandma and I put them in at exactly the right temperature. And besides, I'm a very good cook who never burns things. Aren't I, Grandma?'

'You certainly learn fast, little one.'

'Come on, then.' Fondly ruffling her long fair hair, Jake collected his coffee and followed his happily skipping daughter back into the kitchen.

In the living room, Tilda Larsen sat down beside Ailsa in the seat her son had vacated. Sighing, she proceeded to take the younger woman's slim hand and hold it firmly in hers. 'My son looks happy,' she started. 'At peace with life for once instead of being in a battle with it. My intuition tells me that's because of you, Ailsa.'

Could she *dare* to believe that what she was hearing was true? Once again hope lit within her, and, having learned that Tilda was anything *but* disappointed or angry with her, Ailsa allowed herself to relax and let down her guard. 'It's been—it's been nice spending the past few days together,' she admitted softly. 'And we've talked...*really* talked... for the first time since the divorce. I think that it's helped both of us.'

'That is good...very good. But now, my dear, I am going to speak my mind.' Still holding onto her hand, Tilda gazed steadily into her eyes. 'You should never have divorced. I can see that it shocks you to hear me say that, but please do me the honour of just listening for a moment, will you?'

With her stomach plummeting to her boots, Ailsa grew tense again. 'All right...'

'It was nobody's fault—neither yours nor my son's. You were both so heartbroken that it was a wonder you could make a decision about anything. It was certainly not the time to make a decision to divorce. I knew you were both struggling with your relationship...how could I not when I saw my son so busy with work and not his family? It was the same behaviour that my own husband exhibited throughout our married life. It makes it very hard for a woman to cope. I knew that Jacob loved me, but it didn't come easily to him to demonstrate it. I know that Jake found the way his father was very difficult to deal with. Do you know even on his deathbed my Jacob was worrying about the business—about how our son would handle things? They had clashed many times about the innovations Jake wanted to make. My husband was old school... he believed in learning to do a thing and sticking to that method for the rest of his life.'

Tilda sighed softly, shaking her head. 'After the accident you both needed much more support than you believed. But again—because of your great grief—neither of you was open to receiving it. It grieves me to say it, but in the years since you have separated my son has become a changed man...a man I can't seem to reach no matter how hard I try. It isn't just the tragic death of the baby or the harsh wound on his face that has altered him. Without you in his life, Ailsa, he is like a ship without a rudder. He's become more and more isolated and alone. The only thing that makes life worth living, he told me once, is Saskia. It's only when he's with her that he becomes animated... alive. Now...I am going to ask you something and I want you to tell me the absolute truth. Don't say what you think I want to hear...do you understand?'

Biting her lip, Ailsa nodded. Tears were already swimming into her eyes.

'Do you still care for Jake?'

Retrieving her hand from the older woman's warm clasp, she drew it back onto her lap. 'Yes, I do...very much.'

'Then I am going to make a suggestion.' Tilda's smile was tender as well as infinitely understanding. 'I want you to leave Saskia here with me until Christmas Eve and go and spend some proper time alone with Jake. You tell me you have talked, but I sense there is more to say…I am guessing the most important things of all. Then, on Christmas Eve, you must both come and spend the day here with us. I will make up one of the guestrooms and you can stay as long as you like.'

'What about taking Saskia to the market? I know she has some presents she wants to buy, and I've yet to get her the things she wrote down on her list.'

'Let *me* take her to the Christmas market. It makes sense when she probably wants to buy gifts for her mama and papa. You mentioned the list she wrote?'

'What of it?'

'There were *two* letters in the envelope she gave to Jake, yes?'

Remembering the sheet of paper she'd slipped into her pocket in the car, Ailsa felt her heart start to race. 'Yes… there were.'

'Did he read them?'

'No. He gave the envelope to me.'

'So he has no idea what Saskia wrote on those two pages?'

'I let him read her Christmas list…but that's all.'

'Ahh…'

There was a wealth of knowing in the other woman's softly-voiced response, and Ailsa squirmed uncomfortably. 'I *will* show him the other letter—I really will. But—but the time has got to be right.'

'That is true. Take this chance to be together—just the two of you—and you will find the right time, my dear. That is my advice. Have lunch with me and Saskia, then go home—back to the city with Jake. If Jacob was still here I have no doubt he would give you the same advice. He loved our son with all his heart, Ailsa, even if he often didn't display it. He was so proud of him.'

It wasn't up to Ailsa to tell Jake's mother that he had always doubted his father's love. That was a conversation they would have to have between themselves. But right now, much as she yearned to spend time with her daughter, she knew that the opportunity to be with Jake and finally express her true feelings was not one she should let pass by. No more would she turn and run away from the things that scared her in case they wounded her, or didn't turn out as she had hoped. *In truth, she'd been running away all her life.* Instead, she would face *everything*. If nothing else, she would teach her child by example to be brave in all things.

'Okay. I'll take your advice…providing, of course, that Jake agrees.'

Tilda got to her feet, lightly brushing down the soft folds of the elegant black dress she wore. 'Trust me, my daughter…he will *definitely* agree. To take the chance to spend some important time with you, to talk and rekindle the wonderful closeness you used to enjoy, to try to ease the hurts of the past and hopefully look to make a happier future…why would he refuse? Now, I must go and prepare our lunch or else it will be nearly dinnertime before we eat!'

Jake was strangely subdued as Alain drove them home through the night, back to the town house. They had enjoyed a delicious lunch prepared by Tilda and, afterwards he had gone out into the garden to make a snowman with Saskia. The flakes of white frosting had ceased falling soon after they'd arrived, but it had left a generously thick blanket on the ground. Their little girl had been thrilled that her papa had joined in her play, chasing her and pelting her with lightly fashioned snowballs as she screamed in delight.

It had been a real joy for Ailsa to see them both looking so pink-cheeked and exhilarated by their fun, but now that they had left the magical house in the woods behind Ailsa wondered if Jake was perhaps regretting agreeing to his mother's suggestion that they spend some time together alone over the next few days. The fear she'd been nurturing about him maybe feeling pressurised to rekindle their relationship when he privately didn't want to had worryingly returned. The last thing she wanted was for him to consider them reconciling out of guilt.

To counteract her deep concern, she sought for a safer subject to discuss. 'It was lovely seeing Saskia again, wasn't it? She's clearly very happy staying with your mother.'

'I think it means a lot to them both to be together.' He rubbed his hand round his jaw and gave her a smile...*just*. It was hardly reassuring.

'Are you sure you don't mind us returning home alone, Jake? I somehow get the feeling that you're not altogether happy about it.'

'Let's wait until we get inside to talk about it, hmm?'

Lapsing into an unhappy silence, Ailsa went back to gazing out of the passenger seat window. Staring at the tall shadows of trees and bushes and the snowy landscape that swept past, she clasped her hands tightly together in her lap and wished she could return to feeling more hopeful. Now the journey home felt interminable.

When at last Alain drove the car into the generous-sized private parking space in front of the impressive town house, this time she waited quietly for the polite Frenchman to open the door for her.

'Goodnight, *madame*. I hope you enjoy the rest of your evening,' he said with a smile.

Already at the front door, inserting his key into the

lock, Jake waited for her to join him before going inside, holding the door wide for her to precede him.

'Would you like a nightcap, or a maybe a coffee?'

He took her wool jacket from her to hang it up on the elegant coat stand by the door—but not before Ailsa had quickly retrieved the crumpled piece of paper she'd jammed into one of the pockets. Closing her palm tightly around it, she felt it all but *burn* her soft skin. 'I'll have a coffee, please.'

'Coffee for two it is, then.' Shrugging off the black cashmere coat he wore, Jake left it on the stand and headed across the marble reception area to the kitchen.

She silently followed his tall, dark-clothed figure, trepidation tightening her chest.

Beneath the bright kitchen lighting Jake deftly and silently went about sorting their drinks—carefully measuring out coffee grounds, turning on the gleaming machine that would make it, and setting out the cups and saucers as if he was deliberately taking as much time as possible to gather his thoughts.

As she sat quietly but restlessly at the table, Ailsa remembered that he had suggested only that morning that when they returned from their visit she should move her things into his room. Had he since changed his mind?

'Jake?' Unable to remain silent, or stay still any longer, she rose to her feet, her grip on the crumpled note in her hand lessening just a little, knowing that whatever happened now she would definitely show it to him.

He turned towards her, the bright glare of the lights above his head making his straight dark gold hair gleam as fiercely as she had ever seen it. His deep blue gaze grew wary. 'What's up?'

'About—about Saskia's Christmas present list.'

'You were right. She asked for very little.'

'Yes, she did. But, Jake, there was—there was another request that she made.'

'I know.' His blue eyes glittered, and amid the hurt Ailsa saw conveyed there she was certain she glimpsed anger too.

'You do? How do you know?'

'How do you think? I was with her all afternoon and she mentioned it to me—wanted to know if we'd read her note while we were in England together. Before I could admit that we hadn't, because we were saving it until we arrived here, she asked me whether we were seriously considering what she'd asked and if we agreed—whether we were going to make it happen in time for Christmas? I guessed then that it had something to do with us getting back together.'

'Oh, God…'

The note curled inside her fist seemed to be on fire now and, feeling almost faint with anxiety, Ailsa unfurled it and held it out to Jake.

He took it, briefly read the contents written in bright blue pencil, sighed, and then left it on the steel counter behind him. 'That's quite some request,' he drawled.

'I know,' Ailsa agreed, her breathing feeling tight and constricted in her chest.

She'd promised herself she would face *everything*—but now, when it came down to it, she was terrified that Jake might say it simply wasn't going to happen…that it was an altogether impossible notion and the sooner they told Saskia that her heartfelt wish wasn't going to come true— not in time for Christmas nor in fact at any other time in the future—the better it would be for all of them.

'Why didn't you show me this straight away, when we were in the car travelling to my mother's? You gave me the other note.'

'Maybe I should have done. But I was worried that you might…' Running her hand over her long hair, she made herself return Jake's steady examining gaze with a firmly fixed one of her own, even if inside she was feeling anything *but* steady. 'I thought that it might make you feel pressurised in some way—trapped, even.'

'Couldn't you let me be the judge of that?'

Alisa flinched guiltily. 'I'm sorry. But, although Saskia means the world to us, I didn't want you to feel that you should agree to her request simply to make her happy. *You* deserve to be happy too, Jake… I want you to do the thing that's best for *you*. And if that means you prefer to have the freedom of being a single man, or ultimately that you want to be with someone else, there'll never be any blame or bitterness in my heart towards you. I promise you that.'

'You mean you'd just let me walk out on you like I did before?'

As the words he uttered in his rich, low voice registered in her brain, Ailsa stared at the striking-looking man in front of her in shock. Moving her head from side to side, she barely managed to swallow down the anguished sob that was so close to breaking free. 'I let you walk out because I believed I had nothing more to offer you. And it was near killing me to see you so unhappy.'

'It was a dark time. I don't think either of us was in our right mind.'

'You're right—we weren't. Who would be after such a shattering thing? But if you—if by some miracle you *did* decide you want to stay with me…to try and rekindle what we once had before things became difficult…you do know I can't bear you any more children? I can't give you the son you always wanted?'

The silence that followed this declaration crackled with

the most unbearable tension. But then Jake spoke, and the cramping in the pit of her stomach started to ease a little.

'You gave me a daughter, Ailsa…a beautiful, bright girl with sunshine in her hair and laughter in her eyes…*and* you gave me a son. Thomas might not have survived, but he's still my son and I'll never forget him. Do you honestly believe that the only reason I wanted to be with you was so that you could give me children and not simply because I—?'

He was suddenly in front of her, his hands urging Ailsa's trembling body hard against his. She thought she would melt from the sheer wonderful contact alone but it was what he was trying to say to her that ensured she was utterly rapt.

'Because…what, Jake?' she whispered.

CHAPTER TWELVE

'Can't you guess? Don't you know?'

If his heart pounded any harder Jake was sure it would leap right out of his chest. It wasn't exactly easy to think straight about anything when those bewitching amber eyes were all but making him quake with the need to hold her and kiss her, to quench the thirst for her taste that he never seemed to be free of.

'I love you, Ailsa. I've never stopped loving you and I never will. When you kept Saskia's note from me I was afraid you were totally against the possibility of us reconciling—else why not show it to me? That's why I was so morose on the journey home.'

'Jake, I've never stopped loving you either...even when I agreed to the divorce. I've since learned that real love isn't something that dies—even when tragedy hits like it hit us. It endures even in the face of tragedy.'

She settled her exquisitely soft palms either side of his face as she spoke, and he was suffused with joy at hearing the words he'd never thought to hear her say again.

'I didn't want us to part,' she continued tenderly, her amber gaze glistening. 'How could I when the very idea was like being threatened with a living death? I lost our baby, then I lost *you*, my love.'

'I was confused and desperate to ease the heartache for

us both when I asked you for a divorce. But if I thought it would make things easier then I must have been crazy. I don't know about you, but I was even more tormented when we couldn't be together.'

Covering one of the gentle hands that cupped his face with his own, he turned his mouth towards her palm and pressed his lips there. The rush of not only pleasure but soaring hope that washed over him at the touch of her velvet-smooth skin beneath his lips almost made him lose his bearings for a moment.

'When I saw you again I knew straight away that my feelings hadn't diminished in any way since we'd parted. They'd grown stronger, in fact. When your farmer friend showed up I wanted to hit him for daring to presume he could have what was mine. If that makes me sound jealous and possessive then I make no apology for it. Not now—not ever! Sometimes I think I might die from wanting you, Ailsa. I certainly don't need a miracle to make me decide to come back to you. Marry me. Marry me as soon as we can arrange it. I don't just want to live with you. I don't just want you to be my companion and lover. I want you to be my *wife*.'

'Do you think—? Do you think I could—?'

'What?' Impatience and a frisson of old fear unsteadied his voice. 'Do you have doubts? If so, tell me what they are so I can reassure you.'

For answer her arms came around his waist and, standing on tiptoe, she planted a firm, arousing, near-*incendiary* kiss on Jake's mouth that was clearly designed not just to stop him talking, but to prevent him from thinking altogether. Now it wasn't fear that unsteadied him but desire hotter than the coals in a blacksmith's fire. He just about suppressed a groan. To add to his torment, Ailsa levelled a mischievous grin up into his eyes. It illuminated a face that in his opinion was already *beyond* merely beautiful. He felt as if he was looking straight at the most wondrous view he could ever hope to see.

'I was only going to ask if I could move my things into your room tonight. Would that be all right?'

'What things do you think you're going to need, baby?' Burying his hands in her hair, he stole a long, leisurely hot kiss. When he lifted his head again, he saw with primal male satisfaction the immediate effect of his passionate caress. Her lips were tantalisingly damp, and a little swollen too, and her golden eyes shone brighter than stars. 'You're certainly not going to need any clothes. At least not until tomorrow's lunchtime.'

'Does that mean we're going to stay in bed until then?'

'Damn right, we are.'

'In that case, do you think we might bypass the coffee and simply go straight there now?'

He would have happily demonstrated his intense delight at such an enticing request if the little minx hadn't laid her finger across his lips so that she could continue talking without interruption.

'Oh, and in answer to your proposal…I would *love* to marry you. You and me…we were meant to be together, Jake. I see that now. You asked me about doubts. I can honestly tell you I don't have any at all. Instead I have hopes… *lots* and lots of hopes for us, my love.'

The full moon shone through the uncurtained window, illuminating the fascinating planes and hollows and sculpted firmness of the masculine face that still had such extraordinary power to enthral her—in spite of what some might judge a cruelly disfiguring scar. To Ailsa that scar would always be heroic, and it didn't mar the man she was going to remarry in any way. Only those with eyes that couldn't really see beyond the surface would call his face anything less than beautiful.

She pushed back the lock of tarnished gold hair that so often flopped onto his indomitable brow…just because she could. She had the immediate satisfaction of seeing Jake's arresting blue eyes darken hungrily. Sitting astride his muscular lean body in the bedroom's plush king-sized bed, with its sensuous silk sheets, she thought she might die from the sheer happiness that welled inside her heart. To be this close to him again—to be intimate without keeping her guard up because she knew she could trust him beyond any other person in her life—was *beyond* happiness to her. Her mouth already tingled and throbbed from his devouring kisses, and her body ached in so many delicious places from his tirelessly passionate attentions. In his arms, she'd had the great good fortune to visit another dizzying galaxy *twice* now, and still Jake clearly had no intention of making that enough. Now she ached to deliver some pleasure exclusively for him.

His hand snapped round her wrist as she moved to disengage her body from his. 'What are you trying to do to me?' he growled in protest. 'Can't you see I'm on fire for you?'

'I'm not going far, I promise. I just want to… I just want to…'

Sliding down his body—a body that was well made and fit enough to make any woman crave touching it, whether experienced in the arts of love or not—she started kissing him…beginning with the pink-tipped flat male nipples that were outlined by fine curling tiny gold hairs. The heady mix of musky flavours was like nectar on her tongue. Following her own specially constructed path across his chest and ribcage down over his taut stomach—a path designed to give her lover maximum pleasure and to build the already great tension in him higher and higher—Ailsa used her velvet tongue to the most provocative effect her imagination could devise. She kissed his hard, honed flesh all the way down to his belly button and beyond—to the fine column of dark gold hair that trailed to the place where she had joined her body so ecstatically with his, so that they could be as one...just as she knew their hearts and souls had always been a part of each other.

'Ailsa... For God's sake, have mercy.'

She called a halt to her provocative kissing to gaze up at him. 'You hardly showed *me* any mercy when you drove me half wild just now.'

'You'll pay for this... I'll drive you even wilder when you—'

The full-bodied groan Jake emitted made Ailsa smile even as she cupped him in her hand and, with a feminine satisfaction borne of intimately knowing her man, felt the power and strength of his manhood.

'Is that a promise?' she asked.

Feeling his hand snake round her wrist once more—this time hard enough to impel her body straight back up to his— She let Jake drop both hands to her softly rounded hips and, as her long hair spilled forward over her bared breasts, fill her yet again. And this time he showed not the slightest restraint at driving her just about as wild as a woman hungry for her man could get...

Christmas Eve, Tilda Larsen's house...

Saskia was eagerly helping her mother lay the long polished dining table for dinner. Several of the Larsen family's relatives and friends were expected to sit down with them that evening and the house looked more beautiful than Ailsa had ever seen it. Candles glowed on every windowsill, exquisite crystal vases and pretty ceramic bowls full of flowers sat on every available surface, and everything in sight was bright, gleaming and festive. The silver-grey skies that day had even obliged with another light smattering of snow—not enough to stall their visitors travelling by road, but adequate enough to make the scenery surrounding the lovely woodland house appear utterly magical.

The mouth-watering scent of roast duck that wafted out from the kitchen stimulated Ailsa's tastebuds into realising just how hungry she was. Her body heated when she recalled that over the past few days she'd spent with Jake not a lot of cooking or eating had gone on. It was just as well he had given Magdalena a few extra days off, insisting to the concerned housekeeper that he and Ailsa would manage well enough by themselves. They would eat out as much as possible, he'd told her, so there wouldn't be much need for cooking anyway.

He had been true to his word. They *had* visited some of the city's most exclusive restaurants. But each time they had, more time had been spent simply gazing hungrily at each other across the table than eating the delicious food they'd ordered. And when they had finished dining they'd hurried home to make love...

The sense of wellbeing that had taken over Ailsa's body had the frequent ability to make her sigh contentedly and smile to herself every time she remembered just *why* she was feeling so good. And now the sense of something wonderful about to happen was definitely in the air—and it wasn't simply because it was the most magical season of the year. Every time she glanced over at Jake and caught his eye as he stoked the coals in the dining room fireplace, she saw that he felt it too. They both had surprises up their sleeves, but they wouldn't be revealing them until later.

'Do you think that Father Christmas will bring me a

surprise, Mama? I mean something that I really didn't expect?'

Her little girl's entrancing blue eyes were studying Ailsa intently.

'You mean like another poster of that young movie idol you're so crazy about?' Moving to stand behind his daughter, Jake dropped his hands onto the small slender shoulders, then affectionately kissed the top of her head.

Saskia's cheeks turned crimson. 'I'm not crazy about him, Papa—I just like the movies he's in!'

'Your father's only teasing you, sweetheart.' Finishing her folding of the last pristine napkin, Ailsa grinned at the man and child she loved more than life itself. 'I'm sure you're going to get lots of lovely surprises.'

'Well, I really want to look my best for dinner, so I'm going up to my room to change. Grandma bought me the prettiest red dress *ever* and I want to wear it.'

'Do you need any help, angel?'

'It's all right, Mama, I'm a big girl now. I don't need any help. I'll be back in just a few minutes.' With a furtive little smile at both her parents, Saskia left Jake and Ailsa alone again.

Giving the festively laid table a final scan, to make sure that everything was as perfect as she could make it, Ailsa smoothed her hands down over the dark skirt that she had teamed with the delicate mulberry-coloured silk blouse she was wearing. Just as she briefly lifted the heavy fall of chestnut hair off the back of her neck Jake stepped up behind her and kissed her nape. Then his arms circled her waist. He smelled wonderful. He was wearing her favourite cologne and, coupled with the masculine warmth that enveloped her, it made her heart miss a beat.

'You look ravishing,' he told her, moving round to urge her against him.

'You look pretty edible yourself,' she teased, loving the way the classic maroon sweater and black jeans made him appear so effortlessly sexy and virile just by virtue of being on his hard, honed body.

'Is that a fact?' His electric-blue eyes helplessly turned dark, as they so often seemed to do whenever he was close to her these days. 'Maybe I'll get you to prove that to me later?'

'Don't keep saying such provocative things to me, or I won't be in any fit state to help your mother in the kitchen.'

Jake flashed an incorrigible grin. 'She'll understand. Right now she's over the moon because we're back together. She'll keep the news to herself, of course, until we tell Saskia—but did you hear her singing earlier? Surely you must realise now where I get my supreme vocal talent from?'

Her fingers already affectionately pushing back the rogue lock of shining gold hair that glanced against his brow, Ailsa studied him in earnest. 'I love your voice—I really do. It's just like… Well, it's a combination of fine cognac heated over a flame and rich, dark velvet…at least when you're speaking. But unfortunately it definitely loses its power to mesmerize when you're singing!'

'I didn't realise you had such a cruel streak in you.'

'Baby, I'll never knowingly be cruel to you again… that's a promise.' Her laughter dying away as she examined the haunting male features before her, she tenderly touched her lips to Jake's.

When she drew back he dropped his hands lightly to her hips, his expression serious. 'I don't expect you never to get mad or frustrated with me again—you know that?' he said. 'There's bound to be days when old hurt or resentment might kick in, and days when grief about our son over-whelms you. But when that happens I want to know that you'll talk to me about it and not just keep it to yourself. Is that a deal?'

'It's a deal—but you've got to agree to do the same.'

'Absolutely—I promise. There's something else I wanted to talk to you about. Let's go sit down for a few minutes before the visitors get here, hmm?'

'It's not that I don't want to talk, Jake, but I'm worried about leaving Tilda for too long on her own in the kitchen without any help.'

'Why? Don't you know the greatest help that both of us can give her is for us to be happy again?'

'Okay, then. But just for a few minutes. We'll have all the time in the world to talk later tonight, when we go to bed.'

'Trust me,' Jake replied with a knowing lift of an eye-brow, '*talking* is not exactly what I have planned when we go to bed tonight.'

Heat surging into her cheeks, Ailsa didn't protest. Why would she when she was still thrilled to know that the man she loved found her so irresistible? Their passionate re-union really was a dream come true.

They moved across the elegant dining room to a sump-tuous sofa laden with several luxurious silk cushions. 'I've been thinking about where we're going to live when we remarry. I mean our main home,' Jake said.

'Oh, yes?'

'I know you love the cottage, but I've been mulling over the idea of basing myself in London full-time again. The Copenhagen branch of the company is flourishing, and there are at least two people there who could easily oversee things by themselves for me. But the cottage is too far a commute, and I don't want us to be apart—not even for a day. Anyway, I was wondering how you would feel about moving to the Westminster penthouse for a while? It will only be until we can find something more suitable—something with a good-sized garden for Saskia to play in and nice views—a riverside place by the Thames, maybe? I've asked my business manager to start looking for me. What do you think?'

'Yes, all right. That sounds fine.'

'I know you've got your business established now, but you can always trade online. I could find you some premises near where we live in London, or when we find a suitable house with plenty of spare room you can work from home if you'd prefer that.'

'I said yes, Jake…I agree.'

He stopped talking then, and Ailsa exhaled a long breath—as if she did so for the both of them.

'Just *yes*? You mean you don't have any reservations about making such a move?' His smooth brow creased in puzzlement.

Lifting his hand, she thoughtfully examined the long fingers, with their blunt-cut nails and the still evident scarring that criss-crossed the otherwise unblemished flesh. Her heart squeezed. 'Right now, I'd go to the ends of the earth if it meant I could be with you, Jake—and that's the truth. As much as I love what I do, my craft business isn't my top priority. My family is…you and Saskia. As long as the three of us can be together then everything else has to fall in with that. Like I said to you before…I don't have doubts any more—just *hopes*.'

'If I drank wine I'd raise a glass to that.' Her husband-to-be smiled.

'What's wrong with orange juice?' Ailsa asked softly.

* * *

It wasn't until dinner was at an end that Jake—seated at
the head of the long festively decorated table, with Ailsa
on his right and his enchanting daughter in her poppy-red
dress on his left—finally lifted his glass to make the toast
he'd been aching to make all day.

Knowingly catching his eye, Saskia clanged her dessert
spoon against her drinking glass to get the full attention
of the assembled friends and family who had shared the
delicious food that Tilda had prepared. Seated at the opposite end of the table from her beloved son, Tilda Larsen
gave her granddaughter an approving wink as the child
got confidently to her feet.

'Everybody…my papa would like to say something.'

She sat down again with flaming cheeks and, leaning forward, Jake lifted her slender little hand to his lips
and kissed it. Then he got to his feet, glancing down the
table at the sea of faces now waiting expectantly for him
to speak.

'Christmas is traditionally a very special time for us
all,' he began. 'And although six months ago I very sadly
lost my father, and my mother her devoted husband, I am
certain that Jacob senior would not begrudge me calling
this day extra-special this year.' During the charged silence
that fell, one could have heard the proverbial pin drop. 'It
is extra-special because my darling Ailsa has agreed to
marry me again,' Jake finished.

'You've given me my surprise! Oh, thank you—thank
you! It's the best present ever…better than anything Father
Christmas could bring!' Jumping to her feet, Saskia en-
thusiastically flung her arms round her father, then moved
round to where her mother was sitting, rushing to do the
same to her.

Everyone cheered and got to their feet, clapping hands

and turning to the people either side of them to exclaim their surprise and delight.

Emotion almost overwhelming him, Jake reached for Ailsa as she somewhat shakily stood up too. Echoing the powerful sensations of joy and happiness that flooded his heart, her lovely eyes glistened with tears. Raising his glass, he made the toast he'd been longing to make. 'To the love of my life—Ailsa. You've given me back my life and made me happier than I perhaps have a right to be. I hope you never have cause to regret coming back to me. I'll work hard every day to make sure you always believe your decision was the right one.'

'You don't have to do anything but be the wonderful man you are, Jake. You've given me back my life too.' His wife-to-be deliberately kept her voice low, for his ears only, and there, in front of his assembled family and friends, he kissed her openly and passionately on the mouth...

In the middle of her careful packing of the photographs she would take with her to Westminster, when she and Saskia moved in with Jake, Ailsa lifted one of the latest framed pictures that stood on the living room mantelpiece and sighed. It was a lovely portrait of herself and Jake, taken on their wedding day two weeks ago. The occasion itself had been a quiet affair in the county town's local regis-ter office—nothing like the big wedding they'd had when they'd first got married, nearly ten years ago—but it had truly been the best day of her life. Tilda had flown over from Copenhagen to join them, and Jake's loyal chauffeur Alain and a lovely young woman from the florists who had created Ailsa's bouquet for her stood as witnesses. Saskia had been the most exquisite flower-girl. After the ceremony they had gone to a very charming country house hotel to have dinner.

Smiling, she touched her fingertips to the portrait. Then, carefully wrapping it, she laid it on the very top of the packing case she'd been filling. Straightening, she glanced down with quiet satisfaction at the familiar circle of ravishing diamonds on her finger. *She was Mrs Larsen again.* Even now she could still hardly believe it.

As long as the commute to London was, Jake had temporarily returned to the cottage with his wife and daughter, until they could all move to Westminster together. But they wouldn't even be staying there for long, because his company manager had found them the most wonderful house by the river in Windsor.

Now, noticing the time, Ailsa went to the foot of the stairs and called out to Saskia, who was undertaking some packing of her own in her bedroom. 'I'm just going to start making dinner, darling. Papa will be home soon.'

It sounded like the most normal statement in the world, but it still gave her a thrill to say it. In the kitchen she checked the ingredients for the meal she was making, put the kettle on for a cup of tea, then stood gazing out of the window at the darkening winter sky, her hand absently rubbing her belly. The snow had all but melted now, but the ice in the air still cut like a knife. She grimaced as the sensation of nausea in the pit of her stomach grew a little more intense. Without realising she'd intended to, she depressed the swtich on the kettle to turn it off. All she was aware of was that suddenly the thought of tea made her feel quite sick.

Moving across to the table, she pulled out a kitchen chair and sat down. Still rubbing her belly, she stilled suddenly, calculating in her mind. She'd been suffering from this disagreeable nausea for several days now. At first she'd thought she'd picked up some kind of tummy bug—or perhaps it was just a combination of nerves and excitement because so many changes in her life were happening so fast? *Now it dawned on her that she'd missed her last period.*

She shot up from the chair and started to pace the floor. 'Oh, my God...' she whispered under her breath. 'This can't be happening...it's impossible. I know it's impossible!'

But, despite her impassioned declaration, Ailsa found herself climbing the stairs to her bedroom. From the lowest dressing table drawer—safely put away beneath a colourful woollen shawl that she no longer wore—she withdrew a slim brown envelope stamped with the name of the hospital she'd been taken to after the accident. Dropping down onto the end of the bed, she took out the medical report that she'd only ever read once. The contents were too shattering for her ever to want to look at them again. But now, with her heart thumping heavily beneath her ribs, Ailsa made herself read the report extra carefully.

With shock and disbelief she saw one statement that screamed out at her above all the others: *It is unlikely that Mrs Larsen will ever be able to become pregnant again and carry a child to full term.* It was the word 'unlikely' that jumped out at her most of all. 'Unlikely' was not exactly definitive, was it? That meant that there was a possibility—in her own case a *distinct* possibility—that she might indeed have become pregnant and *could* carry her baby to full term.

Why had she never noticed the word 'unlikely' in the report before? Why had she believed for all these years that she was some kind of hopeless case? When Jake had suggested they'd both been out of their minds after she'd lost Thomas in the accident it had been truer than they'd realised!

She ran across the hall into Saskia's room. Her daughter

was perched on the end of the bed, which was strewn with all manner of colourful clothing. The pink suitcase that lay open in front of her already had several items folded neatly inside it.

'I've got to drive into town and I want you to come with me, sweetheart. There's something I need to buy from the chemist's.'

'But won't Papa be home soon?'

'We can be there and back before he gets home. Come on, scamp…get your coat and boots on and we'll go.'

'Okay—but as long as I can keep packing when I get back.'

'Of course you can. I'll even come and help you.'

At the old-fashioned look her daughter gave her, Ailsa held up her hands. 'Okay…I know you're a big girl now—but sometimes even big grown-up girls need a little help. I know *I* do from time to time.'

An hour or so later Ailsa was in the bathroom, retouching her lipstick, when she heard Jake's key in the door. She'd exchanged the serviceable jeans and sweatshirt she'd been working around the house in for smart black trousers and a cream blouse with broderie anglaise on the bodice and cuffs. She'd brushed her waist-length hair so many times that it positively crackled. Now she was seized with butterflies as she slowly descended the staircase, to find her handsome husband waiting for her with the most stunning bouquet of flowers in his hand. The look in his arresting diamond-chipped blue eyes commanded her attention far more avidly than the glorious bouquet did.

'Well, well, well—what have we here? You're looking particularly ravishing today, Mrs Larsen… Did you dress in that outfit especially for me?' he drawled.

'Yes, I did. They're beautiful…are they for me?' She gazed appreciatively at the flowers.

'They certainly are. Put them on the sideboard there for a minute, will you? I want to kiss you hello.'

Seconds later she found herself enfolded in Jake's arms, luxuriating in the sense of warmth and security and strong male protectiveness she always experienced whenever she leant her head against his chest and he embraced her. 'Mmm…' she murmured. 'You smell nice.'

'A man's got to do his best to keep his woman satisfied—and that includes wearing her favourite cologne.'

Lifting her face up to his at that provocative comment, Ailsa happily received the urgent, hot, hard kiss he gave her. She made a little sound of pleasure as the tips of her breasts tingled fiercely, then drew her lips away so that she could talk. 'The flowers are a lovely surprise. Coincidentally, today I have a surprise for you as well.'

'You do?' He gave her one of his charming crooked grins.

'I do.'

'Well? Are you going to tell me what it is? Or do you intend to keep me standing here in suspense all evening?'

She took a deep breath in, wanting to savour every moment of this time when she would share her momentous news with her beloved husband, knowing that the memory would be written on her heart for ever. 'I'm pregnant.'

'What did you say?'

'I'm pregnant. As unbelievable as it sounds, I really am. I've done a test and everything.'

'But…but how?'

Ailsa smiled. 'Now is hardly the time for me to tell you about the birds and the bees, Jake.'

He held her away from him for a long moment, his

hands curled round the tops of her arms, his expression stunned, as if he hardly dared believe that what she told him might be true.

'I reread the doctor's report I was given when I left the hospital after the accident and it said that I was "unlikely" to be able to get pregnant and carry a child to full term. It didn't say it was *impossible*. I missed that crucial part, Jake. All these years I've believed that I could never have another child and it wasn't true...it wasn't true!'

'What about the part that says you might not be able to carry the child full term? As wonderful—as *beyond* wonderful—as this news is, I don't want you risking your life to have another baby, Ailsa. Just the thought I could lose you makes me go cold.'

'I'm not going to risk my life, I promise. I'll see a doctor as soon as possible. I'll have all the checks, I'll do everything I can to maximise my chances of having a healthy baby and a safe delivery. What do you say to that?'

She anxiously held her breath when Jake didn't immediately reply.

'Do you think it's too soon?' she asked. 'Do you think we should wait until we've been together for a while again...before we have another baby, I mean?'

Just when she thought he might believe just that, his sculpted lips formed the most dazzling, heartrending smile. 'Okay. Okay, this is really happening, isn't it? Tomorrow I'll take the day off and we'll make an appointment with the best damn obstetrician I can find. You'll have the best care—the best treatment that money can buy. And I *don't* think we should wait to have another baby until we've been together for a while...are you crazy? Dear God, Ailsa...what did I ever do to deserve a miracle such as this?'

Pulling her into his arms again, this time Jake held her

as if he never wanted to let her go, and in her mind she told herself that, whatever happened, everything would be all right. It would be all right because she was with the man she loved—this time for good. Whatever fate had in store for them they would face it bravely, hopefully and together—*united* as one…

* * * * *

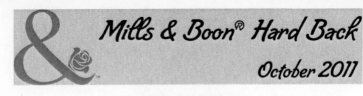

ROMANCE

The Most Coveted Prize	Penny Jordan
The Costarella Conquest	Emma Darcy
The Night that Changed Everything	Anne McAllister
Craving the Forbidden	India Grey
The Lost Wife	Maggie Cox
Heiress Behind the Headlines	Caitlin Crews
Weight of the Crown	Christina Hollis
Innocent in the Ivory Tower	Lucy Ellis
Flirting With Intent	Kelly Hunter
A Moment on the Lips	Kate Hardy
Her Italian Soldier	Rebecca Winters
The Lonesome Rancher	Patricia Thayer
Nikki and the Lone Wolf	Marion Lennox
Mardie and the City Surgeon	Marion Lennox
Bridesmaid Says, 'I Do!'	Barbara Hannay
The Princess Test	Shirley Jump
Breaking Her No-Dates Rule	Emily Forbes
Waking Up With Dr Off-Limits	Amy Andrews

HISTORICAL

The Lady Forfeits	Carole Mortimer
Valiant Soldier, Beautiful Enemy	Diane Gaston
Winning the War Hero's Heart	Mary Nichols
Hostage Bride	Anne Herries

MEDICAL ROMANCE™

Tempted by Dr Daisy	Caroline Anderson
The Fiancée He Can't Forget	Caroline Anderson
A Cotswold Christmas Bride	Joanna Neil
All She Wants For Christmas	Annie Claydon

Mills & Boon® Large Print

October 2011

ROMANCE

Passion and the Prince	Penny Jordan
For Duty's Sake	Lucy Monroe
Alessandro's Prize	Helen Bianchin
Mr and Mischief	Kate Hewitt
Her Desert Prince	Rebecca Winters
The Boss's Surprise Son	Teresa Carpenter
Ordinary Girl in a Tiara	Jessica Hart
Tempted by Trouble	Liz Fielding

HISTORICAL

Secret Life of a Scandalous Debutante	Bronwyn Scott
One Illicit Night	Sophia James
The Governess and the Sheikh	Marguerite Kaye
Pirate's Daughter, Rebel Wife	June Francis

MEDICAL ROMANCE™

Taming Dr Tempest	Meredith Webber
The Doctor and the Debutante	Anne Fraser
The Honourable Maverick	Alison Roberts
The Unsung Hero	Alison Roberts
St Piran's: The Fireman and Nurse Loveday	Kate Hardy
From Brooding Boss to Adoring Dad	Dianne Drake

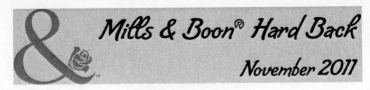

Mills & Boon® Hard Back

November 2011

ROMANCE

The Power of Vasilii	Penny Jordan
The Real Rio D'Aquila	Sandra Marton
A Shameful Consequence	Carol Marinelli
A Dangerous Infatuation	Chantelle Shaw
Kholodov's Last Mistress	Kate Hewitt
His Christmas Acquisition	Cathy Williams
The Argentine's Price	Maisey Yates
Captive but Forbidden	Lynn Raye Harris
On the First Night of Christmas...	Heidi Rice
The Power and the Glory	Kimberly Lang
How a Cowboy Stole Her Heart	Donna Alward
Tall, Dark, Texas Ranger	Patricia Thayer
The Secretary's Secret	Michelle Douglas
Rodeo Daddy	Soraya Lane
The Boy is Back in Town	Nina Harrington
Confessions of a Girl-Next-Door	Jackie Braun
Mistletoe, Midwife...Miracle Baby	Anne Fraser
Dynamite Doc or Christmas Dad?	Marion Lennox

HISTORICAL

The Lady Confesses	Carole Mortimer
The Dangerous Lord Darrington	Sarah Mallory
The Unconventional Maiden	June Francis
Her Battle-Scarred Knight	Meriel Fuller

MEDICAL ROMANCE™

The Child Who Rescued Christmas	Jessica Matthews
Firefighter With A Frozen Heart	Dianne Drake
How to Save a Marriage in a Million	Leonie Knight
Swallowbrook's Winter Bride	Abigail Gordon

Mills & Boon® *Large Print*

November 2011

ROMANCE

The Marriage Betrayal	Lynne Graham
The Ice Prince	Sandra Marton
Doukakis's Apprentice	Sarah Morgan
Surrender to the Past	Carole Mortimer
Her Outback Commander	Margaret Way
A Kiss to Seal the Deal	Nikki Logan
Baby on the Ranch	Susan Meier
Girl in a Vintage Dress	Nicola Marsh

HISTORICAL

Lady Drusilla's Road to Ruin	Christine Merrill
Glory and the Rake	Deborah Simmons
To Marry a Matchmaker	Michelle Styles
The Mercenary's Bride	Terri Brisbin

MEDICAL ROMANCE™

Her Little Secret	Carol Marinelli
The Doctor's Damsel in Distress	Janice Lynn
The Taming of Dr Alex Draycott	Joanna Neil
The Man Behind the Badge	Sharon Archer
St Piran's: Tiny Miracle Twins	Maggie Kingsley
Maverick in the ER	Jessica Matthews